LE CHIEN COUCHANT

As usual, Madame Biron served without uttering a single word. So he did not look up when, half an hour later, she put his dessert in front of him; apple sauce he noted as he folded up his paper, but there was a bottle of champagne beside it. He flushed, then, half rising, called, 'Madame Biron!' in a hoarse voice. She came to the door, still not speaking. He could read nothing in her eyes. Suddenly she terrified him.

'What's up? Why the champagne?' he asked in quick anger. He was all set to fly into a rage, accuse her of having searched his room, but she flashed him a charming smile, a smile such as he had never before seen on her (actually she hadn't ever smiled at him), and said, 'I've had good news today, Monsieur Gueret. I'd like you to share the bottle with me.'

LE CHIEN COUCHANT

Françoise Sagan

Translated from the French by C. J. Richards

A STAR BOOK
published by
the Paperback Division of
W. H. Allen & Co. PLC

A Star Book
Published in 1986
by the Paperback Division of
W. H. Allen & Co. PLC
44 Hill Street, London, W1X 8LB

First published in France by Flammarion et Cie, 1980
First published in Great Britain by W. H. Allen & Co. PLC in 1985

Copyright © Flammarion 1980
This English translation copyright © E. P. Dutton Inc. 1984

Printed and bound in Great Britain by
Anchor Brendon Ltd, Tiptree, Essex

ISBN 0 352 31791 4

To Massimo Gargia

My thanks to Monsieur Jean Hougron for his unwitting co-operation. It was one of the short stories in his excellent collection *Les Humiliés*, published by Stock, that inspired this book: a boarding-house keeper, a repeatedly humiliated man, stolen jewels. Even though I completely transformed both the story and its elements, I wanted to pay tribute to his talent as well as thank him for having stirred my imagination and sent it down unaccustomed by-ways.

F.S.

The book-keeping department had been removed to the rear courtyard, to a small red-brick building – though time had dulled the redness – the only part of the old Samson factory still standing. The view from Gueret's window, as far as the eye could reach, was of a flat landscape broken by a few wretched and deserted miners' cottages randomly situated, some of them half crumbling to dust. But they were still more numerous than the trees – three blighted trees pitched in their midst, in a sad parody of Calvary, in the throes of a slow, lingering death.

The tallest of the slag heaps, the one closest to

Gueret's window, lay between him and the setting sun, so that every evening, as the lengthening shadow slowly stretched from the naked field to the wall of the enclosure, Gueret felt it might spill over the wall and reach the window at which he stood – an optical illusion he found disquieting. Because he had to pass in front of this slag heap as well as two others on his way home, he preferred the winter months when all was dark and there were no shadows to walk through.

'Have you finished doing expenses for the trip to Touraine? No? Oh, pardon me – I see it's already ten to six, and of course Monsieur Gueret's in a hurry to leave.'

True to form, Mauchant had come in on tiptoe and had started barking right away, a procedure which always startled Gueret.

It wasn't that Gueret was worried that Mauchant's hatred might lead to anything, for he knew himself to be so unremarkable, so insignificant, so conscientious that the mere thought of his dismissal was absurd. What troubled him was the completely gratuitous nature of this hatred. It was not the condescending irritation of a boss for an underling; it was something very different. And no one, neither Gueret, nor even Mauchant himself probably, knew why or how it had become so patent and, in a way, so inexcusable.

'Oh, but I have finished them, sir,' said Gueret as he got to his feet and automatically went through the tidy little piles arranged in front of him. His hands were suddenly clammy, his face flushed as he searched desperately for the papers that had been ready three hours ago. He held them out to Mauchant, annoyed with himself for feeling so relieved at having found them.

'Here they are,' he said, his voice too loud. 'Here . . .' But Mauchant had already gone. Gueret stood there, papers in hand. He shrugged his shoulders. The whistle was already blowing, so Mauchant had lied: it was not ten to six but two minutes to six when he had started yelling.

Gueret put on his raincoat with something of a struggle, for the lining of the sleeve was torn; he had been meaning to mend it for the past week.

Outside, though it was warm, he pulled up his collar and walked a few steps to the corner café that bore the unlikely name of the Three Ships. He peered through the window. Inside were the same people who had been there the day before, and the day before that, and who would be there tomorrow: four Samson employees starting their game of cards, two youngsters at the pinball machine, the drunken watchman at the zinc counter, two lovers in the corner, and Jean-Pierre, the morose proprietor who was keeping a jaundiced eye on the new, slightly cross-eyed waitress. Nicole was also there with her constant companion, Muriel. Both of them were looking towards the door. Gueret hesitated, thinking they had seen him. For no particular reason he retreated, sketched a vague gesture of denial addressed to no one in particular, and with assumed haste took off in the direction of the slag heaps.

It had rained during the afternoon. A vaporous sun made the steel and bricks of the landscape glisten. He walked quickly, looking, he hoped, like a man with a purpose. Actually, walking fast released him from the compulsion to do something with his hands; this kept him from thinking about his big, awkward body – which, rightly or wrongly, was the way he had thought of it ever since puberty.

A dog came out of a house at the same time as on other days and started to follow him. Its pace matched Gueret's. Every evening, for some reason, the dog followed him for five hundred yards. It never actually came up to meet him, but somehow their paths would cross. It then followed him, stopping a short distance from Gueret's boarding-house. From there the dog would watch Gueret disappear inside, then turn and go home, loping along somewhat aimlessly.

As Gueret came out of the shadow of the first slag heap, he stopped to light a cigarette. The evening breeze, for the first time carrying country smells and a scent of grass, blew out first one, then another, and finally a third match. The fourth match burned his fingers and, irritated, he threw away the packet before tearing out another. Now that it was too late, the first match caught and burned on the ground where he had thrown it.

Gueret just looked at it. Something glinted in the black coal and he took a step towards it. Whatever it was could just be seen among the pieces of slag; it looked like a chain. Bending down, he noticed it was attached to a heavily embossed watch, which was in turn entangled with yet another chain. Gueret squatted, brushed aside a couple of pebbles, and saw, under the slag pellets, a small tan leather pouch, black with dust. He opened the pouch, which was bulging and heavy. His fingers shook with excitement, as though he knew, even before seeing it, of the treasure it contained: sparkling rubies, rings, necklaces, antique settings – superb jewels that he instinctively felt were genuine. He was so sure of it that he immediately covered the pouch with a handful of stones, to hide it, then looked around guiltily. But behind him there was only the dog looking at him. It had come closer, whining with excitement, wagging its tail at Gueret's find.

'Go away!' said Gueret in a low voice. 'Go away!' For a fleeting moment he thought the dog wanted to take what already belonged to him. He raised his hand in a threatening gesture that stemmed from a combination of fear, pleasure, and suppressed anger and dread of Mauchant. The dog backed away, ears drooping. Gueret pushed back the stones and put the pouch in his pocket.

He got up, his heart thumping, and mopped off his brow. He was trembling and soaking with sweat, but as he looked out over the flat, lifeless little town that knew nothing of his discovery or of his existence, he felt a surge of triumph; his spirits soared and he stretched with pleasure in the sun – a totally uncharacteristic pose. He was rich! He, Gueret, was a rich man! Seized with belated remorse, he called to the dog and for the first time put out his hand to it, tried to pat its head. But the dog had been frightened; its eyes were filled with reproach and it backed away before running home, its tail between its legs. For a second, Gueret thought this a bad omen, but when he strode off he did so with a new bearing: head held high, hands in his pockets, his old tie flapping in the breeze.

The name of his boarding-house was the Wisteria – probably because of the vine that grew around the door. Unlike the rest of the house, it was not smothered with soot, but shone in the sun, a bright green that Gueret noticed for the first time. However much he tried, he could not even for a second imagine his landlady, Madame Biron, in the act of dusting it; that seemed the last thing she would do.

He pushed open the door, wiped his feet, and instead of hanging up his raincoat on the wooden coat-rack in the dreary hall, hugged it to himself. He stopped at the kitchen door, open as usual, and said, 'Good evening', in a flat voice. The kitchen was a large, clean room that might even have been cosy were it not for the unfriendly back of the woman who presided over it: the back of a slender, strong woman with shiny black hair who, when she turned towards the door, showed a totally blank, expressionless face, a face that had seen much in fifty or sixty years and had often been repelled by what it saw. Her inscrutability, and an assumed peasant-like appearance – black apron, heavy shoes – were both out of tune with her intelligent, eager eyes. Just as he had noticed for the first time the green of the wisteria, so now he noticed for the first time the traces of make-up on the face of this woman whom he had thought of as sexless.

She cast him a scornful, weary look and returned his greeting curtly.

He tiptoed up the stairs to his room, a long, narrow room containing a chest of drawers, a bed, a table, a painted wooden chair. A crocheted tablecloth that matched the bedspread, and a small statue of the Virgin under glass on the mantelpiece were the only non-essentials in the room. Gueret opened the window, leaned his elbows on the sill, and looked at his slag heap with a feeling of complicity. In the sunlight, its mass appeared golden to him – but when he looked down, what he saw was Madame Biron's garden with its lettuces, potatoes, and three geraniums enclosed by a fence.

He closed the window, locked the door, took off his raincoat, and emptied the bag onto his bed. The jewels, sumptuous and out of place, sparkled on the crocheted spread. Gueret, sitting at the foot of the bed, looked at them as he might have looked at a woman beyond his reach. After a moment he leaned over and put his cheek on the cold gems. The sun, now rosy in a rain-washed sky, shone through the window, intensifying the brightness of the jewels.

The next day a rickety tram took Gueret into town. He was dressed in his Saturday clothes: a corduroy suit that clung to his big frame. The jeweller in the shop he entered looked at him without interest until he saw the stone – the smallest of the lot – that Gueret displayed with a nonchalant air. Immediately his expression changed.

'It was my mother's only jewel,' explained Gueret hurriedly, looking embarrassed, 'and as we're having money troubles . . .'

'You could get one hundred thousand francs for it,' said the man, 'one hundred thousand minimum. It's a beautiful stone, flawless.' There was a question in his voice, and Gueret, unable to help himself, embarked on an explanation.

'We've had it for a hundred years. . . . My grand-mother . . .' He was still mumbling as he closed the door.

He crossed the square and stopped in front of a camera shop, then, farther on, in front of a luggage store, then, still farther on, in front of a travel agency with colourful posters in the window. His expression was one of intense interest and deep concentration, tinged with surprise rather than greed.

The jewels, wrapped in Kleenex, were still in the rubber boots into which he thrust his hands as soon as he came back. He left the jewels there and stretched out on his bed. He took the sparkling stone out of his pocket and turned it around in the palm of his hand for a long moment before opening the brochures that he had picked up at the travel agency. He looked over the photographs of sunny beaches, palm trees, and hotels.

He normally dined in a small room on the first floor near the kitchen, at the same table as Monsieur Dutilleux, a railway employee, a taciturn widower. When Madame Biron put soup in front of Gueret he commented on the widower's absence. She reminded him that Monsieur Dutilleux often went to see his daughter in Béthune over the weekend. Satisfied on that point, Gueret opened his paper and began to consume his soup. As usual, Madame Biron served without uttering a single word. So he did not look up when, half an hour later, she put his dessert in front of him; apple sauce he noted as he folded up his paper, but there was a bottle of champagne beside it. He flushed, then, half rising, called, 'Madame Biron!' in a hoarse voice. She came to the door, still not speaking. He could read nothing in her eyes. Suddenly she terrified him.

'What's up? Why the champagne?' he asked in quick anger. He was all set to fly into a rage, accuse her of having searched his room, but she flashed him a charming smile, a smile such as he had never before seen on her (actually she hadn't ever smiled at him), and said,

'I've had good news today, Monsieur Gueret. I'd like you to share the bottle with me.'

He sat down again, his hands shaking so violently that it was she who had to uncork the champagne. She looked at him with a smile – an air of superiority, he thought – and they emptied the bottle without exchanging many words, just the two of them in the narrow dining-room.

He did not know what to make of it. He mumbled, 'Thank you, good night,' before returning to his room, where he took the jewels out of his boots and looked around frantically. All the hiding-places struck him as being inadequate. He ended up sleeping with his knees under his chin, the leather pouch under his pillow.

Sunday went by like other Sundays. He viewed a sports programme on television, went to the movies with Nicole, then had dinner at her place afterwards. She didn't see why he didn't stay to make love to her as on other Sundays, but she was more puzzled than humiliated. Gueret was as conscientious in this as he was in other matters.

Monday was a beautiful day. From time to time Gueret, in high good humour, looked happily at his slag heap, which he had for so long misjudged. He got up from his desk at one minute to six, suddenly overcome with a desire to see his jewels. Just then Mauchant made one of his loud eruptions.

'So, Gueret, had a nice weekend? Not too tired? In good form are you . . . eh?'

Gueret did not look at him, but as he was passing behind him to get his jacket, Mauchant stepped back and Gueret bumped into him.

'Watch what you're doing!' shouted Mauchant, but

stopped short as Gueret turned a ferocious look on him and said, through clenched teeth, 'Leave me alone, Mauchant, God-damn it! Leave me alone!' His tone was so fierce that Mauchant, terrified, stopped blocking the door.

Stunned, Mauchant looked through the window and saw Gueret stride down the path that led to the slag heap. The expression on Mauchant's face, a repellent mixture of fury and shame, delighted the young assistant book-keeper who had witnessed the scene, and who smiled happily as he bent over his columns of figures. Mauchant went out, slamming the door.

When he reached the slag heap, Gueret started playing with the dog. He kept throwing the dog a stick, and when the dog retrieved it, Gueret would start prancing in turn. Suddenly he looked as young as he really was. He laughed and called the dog 'Pluto' and 'Milou'; he had even brought a box of crackers, which they shared sitting near the slag heap.

Gueret went home humming. He stopped at the kitchen door and said a cheerful 'Good evening', but the kitchen was empty. He felt unreasonably disappointed. He walked into his room and stopped abruptly. The dreary walls had been plastered over with the colourful ads from the travel agency. Bikini-clad bathers looked down on the crocheted covers. His room was completely transformed. After a few seconds, certain of what he would find, he opened the empty coal-stove and took out the rear baffle; the jewels were there. Strangely discouraged, he restored them to their hiding-place. He sat down on the bed, then immediately got up and ran downstairs. There was still no one in the kitchen.

He ran the whole way to the Three Ships, arriving out of

breath. Nicole was there with Muriel. Spread out on their table was a newspaper with large headlines: 'MURDER IN CARVIN. BROKER SLAIN.' At first this conjured up nothing in Gueret's mind, probably because the word 'broker' suggested to him the world of finance. But the name Carvin made him read on, albeit idly. 'The victim, a man named Gruder, lived in Belgium and was reputedly involved in shady deals . . . He was seen at the border . . .' Suddenly the word 'jewels' leaped out at him. 'The slain man had shown a consignment of jewels to a creditor to stem his impatience. According to the creditor, they were immensely valuable, worth about eight million new francs.'

He turned to Nicole, who was cackling with Muriel, and asked her, 'Have you read this?' He pointed to the article. They clucked in righteous indignation.

'Stabbed seventeen times . . . Horrible, you've got to admit,' said Muriel. 'The poor guy wasn't even dead when the other one threw him into the water.'

'What other one?' he asked automatically.

'The murderer. No one knows who it was. He pocketed the jewels, though, that's for sure.'

'He knew what was in it for him, didn't he?' asked Muriel. 'Eight million francs!' Muriel was more cynical, more stimulating than Nicole, who was simply indignant. Muriel poked fun at her. 'Come on, admit it! Wouldn't you like to have those jewels? Suppose your boyfriend gave you one?' She indicated Gueret with her chin.

Nicole, embarrassed, blushed. 'I'm not asking him for anything.' Her dignity suddenly exaspered Gueret.

'Yes, you are. You're asking me to spend my whole life

at Samson. You'll be at home with the kids and the government family allowances, and I'll be at the office with Mauchant breathing down my neck. That's what you're asking from me!' His throat felt constricted and his voice shook, as though an injustice had been done him. Startled the two girls watched him get up and disappear in the direction of the big slag heap.

When he reached the boarding-house he was glad, then surprised to see Madame Biron at the door. She seemed to be looking at him, but he turned around twice to check: there was no one behind him. It was the first time he had seen her at the door. He stopped in front of her, said, 'Good evening', with a question in his voice, but she looked at him wordlessly, blocking his passage, her expression oddly happy. It took her a full minute to stand aside, then reply, 'Good evening, Monsieur Gueret.'

He remained baffled by her respectful tone even after he saw the newspaper open on the kitchen table.

Dutilleux, the widower, back from the weekend at his daughter's, had spread snapshots of his grandson on the dining-room table. He turned a flushed, laughing face to Gueret. 'Look, Monsieur Gueret, that's my grandson. He's eight days old. Isn't he beautiful?'

'He certainly is,' replied Gueret, embarrassed. 'And that's your daughter?'

'Yes, that's his mother. Not bad-looking, is she, old Dutilleux's daughter?' The old man had had one too many. He alternately sniffled and laughed with delight. Madame Biron indicated with her eyes the bottle of Byrrh to Gueret. She smiled in a conspiratorial way and Gueret caught himself returning her smile.

'Help yourself, Monsieur Gueret,' she said, 'the drinks are on Monsieur Dutilleux tonight.'

'Yes indeed, tonight Grandpa's paying.' The old man hiccoughed. 'You'll see for yourself how cute tiny babies are when you have some of your own. I bet you'll spoil them, don't you think so, Madame Biron? He'll make a good father, Monsieur Gueret will.' Her back was turned, and as she did not answer, he persisted: 'Don't you think he'll make a good father?'

Without turning, she answered, 'Monsieur Gueret doesn't look like a father. You're probably telling yourself that he doesn't look like a criminal either; he looks like a fine, upstanding man!'

'There, you see, my boy,' the old man concluded as he started on his soup.

Understanding finally dawned on Gueret; he was petrified. The woman thought him capable of murder. Of course – he had the jewels, so she presumed him guilty. Why, then, hadn't she called the police? Why had she stood at her door with that motherly expression on her face?

He looked fixedly at her as she approached with the soup tureen. Placing it in front of him, she looked him straight in the eye. Blushing, unnerved, he first pointed to himself, then to the paper, then shook his index finger in a pantomime of denial. Her expression did not alter. She appeared not to take in his mimicry and failed to register surprise. Maybe she was afraid of him now? Did she want him to believe she knew nothing? Was she waiting for him to go to sleep before calling the cops? He simply had to talk to her as soon as the old geezer had gone to bed. But the tipsy grandfather was not to be got rid of easily.

23

'Have you read the item about Carvin?' he asked, rattling the paper. 'What times we live in! To kill a man for a few stones!'

'Yes, but pretty stones! Maybe too pretty,' said Madame Biron.

'Why *too* pretty?' asked Dutilleux.

'Those jewels can be identified. The murderer'll get himself caught trying to sell them. Anyway, who would he unload them on in the first place? He'd have to know the territory.'

So she was also worried about the jewels, Gueret noted. She must have thought that he was trying to peddle them locally and was warning him. So she was not going to turn him in. He felt relieved and vaguely disappointed. There really was no mystery about Madame Biron; she simply wanted a share of the swag, that was all. He was tempted to challenge her.

'Well then, he would have to share. But maybe that's not what he has in mind.'

'He doesn't have any choice,' said the woman curtly. 'With the cops after him, with those kinds of charges against him . . .'

'Listen to this,' said the old man, deep in the newspaper account. 'What a sadist! He stabbed him seventeen times. He can't be human.'

'You think not? A strong man in a rage can do almost anything.'

Madame Biron's tone was detached and – Gueret could scarcely credit it – admiring. So she thought him strong. Well, he was. He stretched out his arm, made a fist, saw the muscle swell under the thin fabric of his shirt, and suddenly derived an unaccustomed new pleasure from it. When he looked up, his eyes met the woman's and he blushed. She was looking at him, at his bulging arm and tight fist, with a sort of sensual respect. He slowly relaxed his arm muscle and fist. All at once he felt weak, empty. He no longer wanted to convince her he was not the murderer; he realized now that he preferred having her look at him with that appalling admiration rather than with her customary disdain.

'I'm going to bed,' said the grandfather, staggering to his feet.

'Help him upstairs, Monsieur Gueret,' said the woman peremptorily. 'He's going to fall.' She was speaking to him as she used to 'before', and Gueret, who had risen to his feet at once when she issued the order, just as he always did when Mauchant spoke, couldn't bear to hear that tone once again; so he deliberately resumed his seat, looking mulish.

'Don't bother, Monsieur Gueret, I can find my bed by myself.' The old man was acting proud, but he stumbled against a chair and his arms flailed the air. Ashamed of himself, Gueret leaped up and caught him as he was about to fall.

'Let me help,' he said. 'I'll put you to bed.'

He hoisted Dutilleux up the stairs, sat him on the bed, and was beginning, with difficulty, to take off his shoes, smiling vaguely at the old man's silly stories, when he heard the click of the telephone downstairs. He stopped, dropped the foot of the poor man, who fell back onto the bed, and rushed to the staircase. As he leaned over the banister, he could see his landlady's lengthened shadow on the linoleum. She was standing by the telephone humming a carefree jazz tune that struck Gueret as ill chosen. He went down the stairs noiselessly. Her back was towards him, but he heard her say in a quiet voice, 'I'm waiting. Yes, I'll hang on, miss. Yes, Biron, 25 Route des Plaines. Yes, it's urgent.'

She was going to summon the cops and he would be sentenced and perhaps even executed for having done nothing. He took a step towards her and caught her by the shoulders in a pleading gesture. Surprised, she turned around and looked at him standing so close to her, but she did not betray the slightest unease. She was speaking with authority into the telephone.

'No, B-I-R-O-N. Oh, hello. You've forgotten my seed order, that's what. When will I be able to plant my nasturtiums? Thursday? Without fail? All right. I'm counting on you. Goodbye.'

She hung up quietly. She had not taken her eyes off Gueret, who was leaning against the wall, trying to catch his breath. Her look was one of puzzled amusement.

'I thought . . .' he began.

'That was the seed store in Béthune,' she explained. 'He ought to have made his delivery ten days ago.'

'I thought you were calling the . . .' He couldn't get the word 'police' out. 'You know,' he said, speaking very fast, 'you know, it wasn't me. I'm not the guy who . . .' With his right hand hip-high he unthinkingly acted out the stabbing. As he followed her eyes, which she had lowered to look at his pantomime, he realized to his horror that he was still holding old Dutilleux's shoehorn. He dropped it as though it had been red-hot.

'That's none of my business,' she replied quickly, in a reassuring tone. 'All that newspaper nonsense doesn't interest me.'

He was stunned. He looked at her, again shamelessly flattered by the deferential tone she had adopted.

'What do you want?' he asked.

She shrugged her shoulders. 'What do I want? I don't "want" anything in particular. It's just that I don't "want" to end up in this hole.' She pointed to the narrow hall, the dark kitchen, and the ill-lit stairwell papered a bilious yellow. 'I'd like to die in a nice place,' she went on, 'a place I like. And first, I'd like to live it up a bit. Do you understand?' Her eyes glistened like a cat's. She looked so avid, so dangerous, that Gueret recoiled. He was afraid of her.

That was the limit. *He* was afraid of *her*.

'Can you understand that, Monsieur Gueret? Don't you feel the same?'

'Oh yes. I'd like to live under a warm sun, surrounded by the sea.' As he spoke he could see coconut palms, surf breaking on a beach, and himself, Gueret, walking about the beach, alone. Always alone.

'I don't give a damn about the sun,' the woman said through clenched teeth. 'You can't buy the sun; the sun belongs to everyone, doesn't it? I want something I like, something that belongs only to me. No one else. Then, whether it rains or shines . . .'

'And if Carvin happened to be where your beautiful place was,' said Gueret indignantly, 'then you'd stay here, too? You'd stay, surrounded by all this?' He pointed to the landscape that was no longer visible now that night had fallen, the sinister landscape which he regarded as a personal insult – now that he could leave it.

'When you're rich you can keep your windows and doors shut,' she replied severely. 'You don't have to see

27

anything except the end of your toes if that's what you want. And to while away the time, you can even have your toes massaged for hours on end, by flunkies who are paid to do just that.' Her voice had changed; she raised towards him a face that was suddenly rejuvenated. 'And the rest of the time you take care of your flowers. Come and see.'

She made Gueret open the door and pulled him into the night. He tripped over the low wire fences she had put around her flower beds. The dark mass of the slag heap stood guard against an absurdly bright sky. 'Look,' the woman said, bending down. 'Use this lighter. You see those peonies over there? I planted them six years ago. They were almost grey the first time they bloomed. It took six years to make them red. They're beautiful now, aren't they?'

There was no way he could distinguish the colour of the flowers, but she went on, 'First of all, they need a hothouse. A huge hothouse with streams of water and even heat. It isn't just orchids that – ' She stopped in mid-sentence. She stood motionless next to him, her profile turned towards the flatlands and the slag heap. For the first time he saw a dreamy look on her face. Gueret was in his shirt sleeves, and he shivered in the evening breeze. As though awakened, she turned to look at him.

'Well, now.' Her voice was husky, anger and gaiety mingled in it. 'You're not going to catch cold?' Before he could respond to either her familiarity or her gesture, she had taken off her shawl and bundled him up in it with a little laugh he thought condescending. He made a gesture of rebellion. Did she or did she not think him guilty?

Since when did criminals catch cold so easily? He threw the shawl on the ground.

'I don't want your shawl. And suppose I don't want your hothouse either, any part of it? Those dumb things cost a bundle to build. Why don't you just take it all while you're about it.'

'Yes. Why not?' she replied with a tight little laugh. She picked up the shawl from the ground and brushed it off with her hand. It was black with mud, and Gueret wanted to apologize, ask for forgiveness, like a bad-tempered child. Too late!

'Well, if war is what you want, that's what you'll get,' she said as she turned her back on him. And before going into the house she turned around. Her voice was harsh: 'And don't try to play it smart, Gueret, will you? If something happens to me I've got friends who'll know what to do.'

It took him a few seconds to recover before he forced out a manly and scornful laugh. But even as he did so, he still tingled with the newly discovered pleasure of rebellion.

He climbed the stairs with a heavy tread and slammed his door. He stood in front of the mirror looking hard at himself for at least a minute before stuffing his hand into the pocket of his jacket. With his thumb he aimed an imaginary gun and in a low voice spat out insults and orders at his own reflection. His face quickly reassumed its customary air of defeat and embarrassment, but this time mingled with disbelief at the challenge of this unconvincing gangster. Gueret then moved closer to the mirror, looked at himself with interest, this time without making faces. With his left hand he smoothed his hair, flattening it against his forehead, and looked serious. Suddenly, for the first time ever, he thought himself almost handsome.

Early the next day it was not Gueret the book-keeper but Gueret the notorious gangster who went through the doors of the Samson firm. Sensing a change, his fellow employees watched him walk by, then turned around to look at him. The top button of his shirt was open, his tie loosened. His large body moved decisively, without a trace of heaviness or clumsiness. And for the first time also the women in the factory thought him handsome.

He pushed open the door to his office and settled down at his table without answering the glum 'Good mornings' of his fellow workers, instead merely making a gesture.

'Like a pop singer on TV,' said young Jonas, the assistant book-keeper. The first thing Gueret did was to shove his chair back from his table, lifting his eyebrows in surprise at the exiguity of the space allotted him. He then firmly pushed his desk one yard forward, thus encroaching on the territory of Promeur, the assistant head book-keeper. The latter, who was deep in calculations, started: he shot an incredulous, then outraged, look at Gueret.

'Hey, Monsieur Gueret, just where do you think you are?'

The two trainees looked up, delighted at the diversion. Gueret, still saying nothing, put wedges under the legs of his desk on the conquered territory. He went to the window and opened it wide, letting in a broad ray of sunshine and a breeze that scattered papers.

'He's gone crazy!' Promeur shouted as he ran after his papers. 'Monsieur Mauchant will hear about this, let me tell you!'

But even invoking Mauchant's name didn't seem to bother the apparently demented Gueret, who was now openly laughing at his colleagues scrambling about on all fours. Perched on a corner of his table – like Humphrey Bogart, the young apprentice noted again – he lit a cigarette, his left eye closed. Once order was re-established, but with the window still open, the hour-long silence that followed was broken only by the sighs and indignant grunts of old Promeur, who was obviously waiting for reinforcements.

Mauchant came in at the usual time, pushing open the door with his elbow. He stopped in front of the open window and his complexion became even ruddier than usual.

'What's going on here?' he spluttered, looking furiously at the impassive Gueret, but ostensibly addressing Promeur, the man in charge. The denunciation came promptly.

'It's him!' Promeur bleated, pointing an accusatory finger at Gueret, who, instead of losing his assurance, smiled placidly.

'What's this?' shrieked Mauchant, conscious of the righteousness of his cause and of Gueret's guilt. *'What's all this?'* Baring his teeth, he turned towards the culprit, but the latter was lounging in his chair, his long legs stretched out.

He answered in a voice just as loud as Mauchant's: 'This is fresh air. Oxygen, Monsieur Mauchant. There is a law against suffocating workers, a law against pollution, Monsieur Mauchant, pollution and abusive language! Didn't you know?'

And as Mauchant, who by now had turned purple, took a step towards him, the normally retiring Gueret got up and, towering head and shoulders over the assistant manager, escorted him with a firm hand back to the door.

Events unrolled in the same vein at noon at the Three Ships, where the timid Gueret, letting it be understood that he had won a bet, treated everyone in the café to a round of drinks. He laughed loudly and Nicole even observed him pinch Muriel, which he did with a cocky expression she had never seen before. For the rest of the day the once diffident Gueret strode through the factory in his old tan woollen jacket, his tie loosened, humming, looking free. And indeed Gueret did feel free, young, and triumphant. He did not admit even to himself that it was not really the admiration of the office boys or the new way some of the women looked at him or the compensation for past humiliations that had given him the biggest thrill on this memorable day; it was the look of terror, the wild desire for flight, he had caught in Mauchant's eye as soon as he had risen to escort him to the door.

Near the slag heap he found the dog, who came to meet him barking and prancing with joy. This time it did not back away when Gueret caught it by the collar and petted it. The dog realized he was no longer afraid, thought Gueret: it must have been the fear the dog sniffed on Gueret that had made the animal run away these last days. Seated in the shade of one of those ragged trees that had miraculously grown in the ashy soil, he shared a sandwich with the dog. Later, this peaceful scene was to recur in Gueret's mind as being the moment of his deepest, most genuine happiness: the dog, the dark shadow of the slag heap outlined on the sunny surface of the field, the smell of bread and mustard, and the blinding, friendly sun. Until that moment he had not thought of basking in its warmth, but now, reminded of the pictures in Nicole's magazines and in the folders from the travel agency, he longed to feel it on his body. When the dog left him at the usual place it was from a happy man that it parted; and it was a happy man who went home to his landlady.

But Madame Biron was on the warpath. Drunk with success and having forgotten the war, Gueret had found it easy after work to linger in the café and in the field – but only because he was sure he would find again, in that wretched boarding-house, the look which the night before had given birth to the new Gueret. That look was the very mainspring of his new self. Subconsciously he had come home to seek confirmation of this and to find renewed strength. But there was nothing now in Madame Biron's eyes; for her both the dangerous gangster and the miserable boarder had ceased to exist. She didn't look at him; she hardly saw him.

On the table were cold soup, ham, and potato salad, and one third of a rice cake that old Dutilleux, who was obviously suffering from a devastating hangover, was finishing off. Silence reigned. The late-comer's clarion-like 'Good evening' had been answered by a grunt. Gueret joked about his lateness, started recounting his exploits of the day, then noticed he had no audience. His initial reaction was annoyance, then fury – as if he had brought home a good report card and had been greeted by parental indifference. Nonetheless he said with pride, 'I told that pig Mauchant where to get off.'

But the woman gave him a look of such scorn and irony that he was deflated all at once. His immediate thought was to regret having boasted about putting down such an insignificant little pipsqueak. He ought to have done it four years ago; and there certainly was no call to slap himself on the back, as though he had performed an act of valour. Some exploit for a man who had supposedly stabbed a Belgian businessman seventeen times and thrown him alive into a canal! For the first time Gueret felt a trap closing. He was suddenly afraid that Madame Biron suspected his imposture. He realized that what he was afraid of more than anything, more perhaps than of a possible arrest – and especially now after this day of glory – was that she no longer believed him guilty. He was afraid that the pitiless image of himself as a criminal would fade from her clear, feline eyes. It was that image which all day had allowed him to live like a man. But if the murderer was found? The real one? Supposing she realized that it was only chance, not the anger of a 'cruel and strong man', as she put it, that had put the jewels in his hands?

He realized dimly that that would change everything, that the money she so obviously wanted would lose three-quarters of its value for her; that if the banknotes were not stained with the thick blood of a murdered man, they would become 'unclean' in the eyes of this woman.

Paralysed by this sudden insight, he remained for a second with his fork in mid-air, head bent, bereft of appetite and thought. Old Dutilleux didn't utter a word. She waited on them soundlessly, without making any of the brief comments she occasionally addressed to them.

Gueret slowly fell apart. He carefully buttoned up his shirt, straightened his tie, dropped his fork, became jumpy. He was under the impression that he was chewing too loudly. His hand, his arm, the muscles of his arm felt numb, useless.

When Dutilleux left after a grumpy 'Good night', he felt like calling him back and suggesting a card game, or even getting him started on the campaign of 1940 and his days as prisoner of war, his excruciatingly dull, favourite topic of conversation. But Dutilleux, feeling nauseated, was in no mood to linger. Soon Gueret was alone at the table, heavy and tense, his hands resting on either side of his plate. He was torn between a shamed distress and the yearning to ask for help, but of whom? This impassive woman was like a wall. He could remember now, as in an impossible dream, the few moments when she had laughed, talked about orchids, the sun, her big toe to be massaged by flunkies; the moments during which he had seen in her a vibrant youth, charm, and astonishing beauty.

'I liked her,' he said to himself with surprise, though the surprise was less acute than his regret at being no longer under her spell. Yet that apparently shapeless body, the hair tightly pulled back, the black apron, the inscrutable face etched by time and bitterness, all this was henceforth to be the very picture of his fate. He dizzily dreamed up a wild scenario: he would run upstairs and fetch the leather pouch, empty its tangled contents onto the shiny kitchen table, give them to Maria, even beg her to take them. In a crazy continuation of his dream he saw himself kneeling at the feet of this sad and ferocious housewife, of offering her his life, his blood, his jewels, anything to get her to look at him again with that mystery-laden air of respect and desire. Of course, it wasn't a matter of having her love him, he thought – tried to think; it was a matter of her noticing him again, of her admiring him, and of his attracting her as a male and hero. And now she was refusing him that vision of himself as male and hero – he had never before thought of himself as such, nor had Nicole ever regarded him in that light. The image of himself reflected in Nicole's attitude was wholly devoid of charm and mystery.

The woman was silently, unobtrusively doing the dishes. Suddenly he could stand it no longer; he crashed his fist so hard on the table that his plate bounced right onto the tiled floor, where it broke. She was standing with her back to him but did not flinch; she barely turned around.

'For God's sake!' said Gueret. 'Can't you say something? What have I done? I'm sorry about the shawl, I didn't do it on purpose . . .'

She gave no answer and, bending down painfully – with exaggerated effort, he thought – swept up the pieces with a brush and dustpan. She was deliberately making herself out to be older and more weary than she actually was. She no longer wanted to attract him; she was rejecting him. He tried to pretend that it could make no possible difference to him. For God's sake! What could it matter to him that a brutal, daft, predatory woman gave him the cold shoulder? He would give her a share of the loot, a third or half if she wanted, and with the remainder he would retire to Senegal or elsewhere and live in peace. What more did she want? he kept asking himself incoherently, as though she ought to have known that he had already given up the fight and the ransom.

'The broken plate will cost you three francs fifty, Monsieur Gueret,' she said. 'I'll put it on your bill.'

'I don't give a damn about the three francs fifty!' he said, striking the table even harder with his fist to emphasize his words, hoping the table would collapse, that everything would splatter on the floor and break, that such irreparable damage would finally kindle some spark in her lifeless eyes. But this time nothing moved and he hurt his hand. He put it to his mouth without realizing how childish the gesture was.

'I've hurt myself,' he said weakly, sulkily, as though he could expect some compassion from her. But she was hanging up the tea towel, raking ashes in the stove. She took off her apron and folded it without looking at him, as though he wasn't there. She was going to go up to bed, leaving him alone and vanquished on this lamentable tiled battlefield.

However, he did not dare move when she went out of the room. He sat there for over five minutes after she had left. Motionless, hands on the tablecloth, powerless and desperate, he listened to the ticking of the clock.

When he returned to his room he did not lock the door; he went to the coal-stove, put his hand in, and felt the pouch but did not bother to pick it up. Without undressing, he stretched out on the bed, and chain-smoked until daylight, while in the electric light that was gradually neutralized and made ludicrous by the dawn, the colour photos of Mediterranean beaches and their alluring pin-ups on the wall turned grotesque and terrifying.

It rained the next day and the next. The discreet silent book-keeper had reverted to type. The dog had again taken to running away. On the third day, as Gueret picked up a stone to hurl at a blackbird that was making too much noise at the top of a tree, the dog mistook it for a threat and ran home howling, its tail between its legs. At that point Gueret, alone once more, started to run towards the house, prepared to do something, anything. He went in like a madman shouting, 'Madame Biron! Madame Biron!' in a voice filled with distress and panic, charged into the kitchen and the small pantry, both of which were empty, went without knocking into Dutilleux's room. It, too, was empty. He went into his own room, not even glancing at the stove and its treasure, then without pausing burst into her room.

She was standing in the dark alcove that served as a

dressing-room. Her bathrobe was open, revealing bare shoulders; her hair was loose; she had the vulnerable look of a woman getting dressed. He did not see in the mirror the amused smile, the look of triumph that flitted over her face as he threw himself on her and took her in his arms with the clumsiness of a drunk or an adolescent, burying his face in the nape of her neck and in her shoulder, which was still soft and round, a shoulder that from the back was irresistibly sensual and desirable. She seemed to be offering it to him as if it were his last and only chance.

At daybreak, his torso naked, he sat on her bed and looked through the open shutters as a grey, gloomy light spread over the colourless earth, on which rain continued to beat with a soft, peaceful sound.

She was stretched out behind him, the sheet drawn up to her chin, half-hidden by the pillow. She stroked his back dreamily, almost as if stroking the side of a horse, with a hand that had become beautiful and possessive during the night. He did not stir, so she sharply pinched the skin of his back, but still he did not turn around; instead he simply leaned towards her with a sheepish and satisfied smile. He could not see her in the shadows, but he could hear her voice, the warm, familiar voice of a woman satisfied with her man.

'You're quite a guy,' this voice was saying, 'yes, you're quite a guy.' With her fingers she drummed a tattoo on his side, still with the gesture of a horse trader, and he smiled, looking pleased and flattered. He lit a cigarette simply, without any flourishes, and when she slapped his back imperiously, he offered it to her before lighting another for himself.

'Kind of you to light cigarettes for your old woman,' the jeering voice behind him said. 'You know I could easily be your old mother, don't you, my little bastard?'

He stirred slightly; his features became pinched, but the voice went on, both soothing and ferocious: 'A nice young man who lights cigarettes for his old mum – his tired old mistress. A nice young man who's polite to Monsieur Mauchant, the head book-keeper. A nice young man who thinks nothing of stabbing a poor guy seventeen times in the dark. You know, you're really something.' She started to laugh.

The only indication he gave that he had heard was to look out of the window as he puffed on his cigarette. He felt utterly carefree. He had reached a level of security, a haven in which he was impervious to the taunting, savage voice of the woman behind him, who was quite unconscious of his withdrawal. He even smiled furtively, as if at a private joke, at a trick he might be playing on her. He remained perfectly still as her voice, which had become throbbing, pressing, began to whisper: 'How did you do it? The first three stabs I can understand, but afterwards? How could you? Tell me!'

'No, not that,' he said.

He tossed his cigarette out of the window and turned towards the woman, whose presence he felt rather than saw. He threw himself on her with an anguished fury that was akin to desire.

'What a brute, what a dirty brute,' the woman's voice went on, and then was still.

The following Sunday was a bright sunny one, and the churchbells of Carvin were pealing. Madame Biron, the boarding-house keeper, in her customary black clothes, was watering her flowers, while her lodger Gueret, barefoot in T-shirt and trousers, sat in the doorway, looking at her, a mug of coffee in his hand and the neighbour's fickle dog stretched out at his feet. 'The picture of married bliss,' said the town gossips, dressed in their Sunday best as they went past the house hurrying either to answer the summons of the bell or to flee the indecently peaceful spectacle of their neighbours.

'Don't you think your flowers have had enough water?' asked the young man. 'It's been raining for ten days. Ever since we saw the dawn together,' he added suggestively.

But the woman, busy with her flowers, shrugged.

'It's true,' Gueret went on. 'It didn't stop raining that evening; it rained all night. We heard the rain all night long, don't you remember?'

The woman looked at him somewhat askance, but smiled. 'That's all you ever think of, isn't it?' she said, evincing some curiosity. 'Men are funny; either they don't think at all or that's all they think about . . .'

'And you don't think about it enough,' he reproached her affectionately.

'That's from doing it too much too often, my dear, and with too many fellows. I'm not as young as you, you know.'

Looking resigned, he mumbled something. Then: 'Do you think that letter will get here tomorrow?'

She had gone around the tiny garden and now came back and set her watering-can down in front of him. She stood there, dominating Gueret, looking down at him possessively, with an air of detached satisfaction. He looked up at her with a mischievous smile.

'Maybe not tomorrow,' she said, wiping her hands on her apron.

He took her hand automatically; she left it in his for a moment as though it were an object, then she looked towards the flatlands, the slag heap, and, in her mind's eye, the eventual arrival of the postman. 'But I'm sure by the day after tomorrow. Gilbert moves quickly, he's just got to contact people in Marseilles, that's all. They don't hang about there.'

'You miss Marseilles, don't you?'

'Yes.' Her face was a blank. 'If it hadn't been for that jerk, I'd never have left Marseilles. I love the climate. The colours are so bright there and the people are alive. Marseilles is a real city.'

'Why didn't you ever go back?' Gueret was examining the still hand he held in his own. Their hands, he thought, looked about the same age. He leaned his forehead against his mistress's firm legs.

'Because I'm wanted there,' she said tersely. 'Why are you leaning against me like a kid? You think I'm your nursemaid, Al Capone?'

He shrugged his shoulders without changing his position. In a voice smothered by the black apron he said, 'I feel safe and comfortable.'

'You're not going to tell me your mother walked out on you when you were a baby?' She spoke unsmilingly. 'The unhappy childhoods of pimps and killers are more than I can take.' She made an eloquent gesture.

'My mother was a decent woman,' he said slowly. 'Near the end she was stingy and nasty, like an old magpie, but I wasn't unhappy.'

'Good for you.' She wiggled her hips as if to shed something, and indeed Gueret's head wobbled back. 'Have you found your island?' she asked on her way to the door. 'Or are you still set on Dakar?'

'No. I've made up my mind. We'll go to the Congo. They've got opportunities down there, things to do. The people aren't easy to deal with, but I'll manage.'

His confident smile faded as soon as she was in the house. He looked furtively around and as soon as the blaring radio indicated she was in the kitchen he leaned

down and pulled the dog's head towards him, put his
arms around its neck, and slowly, gently, with great
tenderness, kissed the filthy black coat and shiny muzzle
of the mongrel, who submitted ecstatically to all this
loving.

'Tomatoes or cucumbers?' she yelled from the house.

Firmly but gently Gueret pushed away the dog's head
before replying, 'Either – I don't give a damn.' He lit a
cigarette, his eyes half-closed, à la Humphrey Bogart.

One week later, Gueret was in a large sports shop. He
was an obviously unimportant customer, and the
salesmen kept bumping into him, but he didn't even
notice. In the mirror he could see Madame Biron next to
him – Maria to him now. Her black coat with its otter
collar had clearly seen better days. She smiled at
Gueret's look of excitement and also did not notice at
first the disgusted look of the salesman with the
brilliantined hair.

'Have you seen anything you like? Let's get something
special, don't you think?'

Gueret replied absently, 'Uh-huh, of course . . . But
just look at that machine over there.' He was pointing to
a huge, shiny Yamaha.

The gesture provoked a sneer from the young
salesman, probably in a hurry to leave for lunch. 'No,
sir,' he said loudly, 'that doesn't look like your
department. If I'm not mistaken,' he went on with
malevolent glee, 'your department . . . what you're
looking for . . . is something more like . . . a moped.' He
smiled at his own wit. Other customers were beginning
to smile at this odd couple all decked out in their Sunday

best. Maria noticed it a second before Gueret did, and, letting go of his arm, spun around, her face white with fury. When he saw her eyes, the salesman instinctively recoiled, but it was too late.

'This gentleman may be looking for mopeds,' she said articulating loudly, 'but what I'm looking for is a courteous, pleasant salesman. I'm sure we can find one elsewhere.'

Gueret was nonplussed. She tugged at his arm and the salesman started to mumble. The customers were now staring at him.

Gueret followed Maria to the pavement outside, where she suddenly stopped. She was pale and spoke without looking at him, through her clenched teeth. 'That little jerk,' she spat out, 'that rotten little . . . You go back in there and buy that motorcycle right away. The big Japanese one.'

'But what with?' Gueret was stunned by the sudden fury, which he did not understand. Being pushed around was a way of life to him. Now all of a sudden he was annoyed with himself for being such a drip. He stuck out his chin and muttered, 'OK, I'll deal with him,' but even then he was resisting the push she was giving him. 'But where am I supposed to get the money? And can you see me arriving at the plant riding that? You've got to be joking . . . and anyway, it costs thirty thousand francs. Have you got that much?'

Suddenly she came to. She looked at him and forced a smile.

'Not quite. But I do have a little money in the bank. Sorry, I don't know what got into me . . . Can you stand that sort of thing? Did you hear the way he spoke to you?'

At this point Gueret regained his poise; putting on a stony expression and shaking his head slowly, as he dimly remembered Edward G. Robinson doing in an old film, he said quietly, 'No, I didn't see him. I don't see that kind of guy.'

Already she was hurrying on. She walked fast, and despite his size he had a hard time keeping up. He was panting when he finally sat down next to her in a neighbouring café.

'One cognac,' Maria ordered peremptorily. As in the store, so here the tone in her voice produced miracles; the waiter returned at once, glass in hand. She swallowed it in one gulp without looking at him, while Gueret, not used to drinking in the morning, reluctantly ordered a second one for himself. Maria's breathing had calmed down, her colour was returning; she emptied the last drops in her glass, put it down, and said, 'That's better', before looking at him in a way he had never seen before; hesitantly, sheepishly.

'I don't know what got into me,' she repeated. 'Don't hold it against me, it's the' – she made a vague gesture – 'it's the real me coming out. Do you understand? What rotten luck,' she went on in a steadier voice, 'all my life I've been proud.' (As she said the word her voice still vibrated with that pride.) 'I'm proud and bad-tempered,' she concluded, looking at him defiantly. But Gueret, sitting next to her, smiled beatifically. Now that it was over, he was delighted with the incident, the easy victory, his mistress's strength. People at nearby tables stared at the incongruous couple, but Gueret was totally oblivious to their puzzled interest. Maria, intercepting his admiring look, was flattered by it. She preened herself and once more held her head high.

'Well, you've got to admit . . . just look at us,' she admonished him pleasantly. 'It's not surprising those salesmen didn't take us seriously, all decked out like we are. We really do look like a couple of country bumpkins. We reek of the country – of coal, hay, dung, the works.' She stopped for a moment and with just one look at the waiter ordered another cognac.

'I wanted to lunch at Le Trois Épis,' she said, her anger returning. 'I hear it's the best bistro in town; it's famous for its quenelles. But can you see us eating their quenelles in these clothes? Can you see the headwaiter looking us up and down, me, Maria from Marseilles, you, the mystery man from Carvin?' She had lowered her voice, but Gueret, worried, looked around.

'Come on,' she said, leaving a ten-franc bill on the table. 'Come on, my friend, I'm going to dress you properly.'

They went to a series of department stores, where Maria gave the orders and made the decisions. She seemed to know exactly what she wanted. Gueret scowled; he was going to pay her back, of course. Since the smallest of his gems could buy an entire department store, there was nothing to worry about. But he was embarrassed to be so obviously at a woman's beck and call. In the last store they went to, he came close to blowing his top when a young saleswoman said admiringly to Maria as he was trying on a blue suit, 'Blue is certainly your son's colour.'

Maria, eyes alive with laughter, entered into the joke.

'Oh, my little boy is so strong,' she said to the saleswoman. 'And the tricks he plays on me! Would you believe it, but at almost thirty he's still *growing*? I've been letting out his clothes since he was seven.' And as the young woman gushed politely, she went on, 'And that's nothing; if you'd known his father, miss. Such a handsome man!'

She smothered a laugh while Gueret looked at himself in the neon-lit mirror; he saw a silly overgrown young man rigged out in what looked to him like Sunday best. Silly, yes, and he, too, began to laugh. He had not laughed like that in a long time. As a matter of fact, he could not remember ever having laughed like that; not even when he was doing his military service had he laughed as much with anybody.

At about one o'clock they were at Les Trois Épis for lunch, all dressed up in their new clothes. The headwaiter was deferential, attentive, probably more impressed by their gaiety than by their elegance. There was a look of triumph about them, and that, at any level, tends to induce respect.

Maria ordered grilled lamb chops, well done, and a glass of wine for her son and, before the uninterested headwaiter, dredged up childhood reminiscences which were outrageous, heartlessly commonplace, but which brought to Gueret's habitually suspicious eyes a look of irrepressible mirth. They ate hungrily, and as they were having coffee, Maria, finally sated, her cheeks rosy and her eyes sparkling, gave him a look that was slightly more possessive and less maternal.

'Why does the idea that I could be your mother make you laugh like that?' she asked.

'You should have known my mother!' he said, again choking with laughter. 'She was tiny, skinny, an old mouse.' He laughed again, and although he was no longer hungry, he absentmindedly picked up and swallowed the honey-coloured breadroll on the side of his plate. 'Leave that alone,' she said, rapping his fingers, 'you'll get fat.' She went on in the same tone, 'Stop and think a minute; would you have liked me for a mother?'

'You bet!' Gueret replied with a salacious look. 'I wouldn't have let you out of my sight.' And he laughed again, an end-of-the-meal slightly tipsy laugh. This irritated Maria.

'I'm serious,' she said. 'Anyway, I'm sure I'd have beaten you a lot.'

'Why?' asked Gueret, his interest suddenly aroused. 'Why beat me? What for – to punish me? Why? Because I wanted to be a gangster? An egghead? An Olympic champion? A . . . what? What would you have wanted me to be?'

She pondered for a moment before replying. The restaurant was now empty. They were alone, and from a distance, amid the padded white of the tablecloths, their dark clothes shone in all their new splendour. Her face was flushed – more so than his – which highlighted the grey in her hair. They whispered in a conspiratorial way, their heads close together, gazing at one another with looks alternately hostile and fascinated.

What was disturbing about this couple was not the difference in age but the similarity of type. In this provincial gourmet restaurant, they looked not so much like mother and son, but like a breed apart.

'Oh well,' she said as she stretched ungracefully (swearing under her breath because, as she did so, the sleeve of her new blouse split at the seam). 'Oh, well, whores always seem to get moral when they have kids, haven't you noticed? And the more whoring they do, the more they want their kids to be priests. That's the way. No – what I'd have done is see to it that you made lots of money.'

'How?' he asked. 'By studying, or something else?'

She burst out laughing. 'Have you ever heard a tycoon talk about his miserable beginnings? Did he ever say he got his money from studying? Come on. Kids who are poor don't take courses in how to get rich – there are no courses for that. All they get told is they need money and plenty of it if they're ever going to lift themselves out of the muck. There's no formula, it's do-it-yourself.'

He was looking at her attentively as she spoke. She was intelligent, he said to himself, perhaps more so than he. He wondered at how little it cost him to admit that. He felt completely at ease in this restaurant, which was too shiny and too warm and which ordinarily he would simply have been in a hurry to leave. Every now and then the thought that she had been taken for his mother made him want to laugh again.

'OK, what would I have done?' he said idly, just to prolong this moment of profound peace.

But then he had to assume a tough look when, eyeing him directly she said in a low voice, this time without a vestige of gaiety, 'You found out without any help, all by yourself, didn't you?'

And she turned the knife on the tablecloth in a slow gesture that horrified Gueret.

Every evening, after old Dutilleux had finally gone to bed – a departure they speeded up by yawning and making fake exits – they would meet again in front of the fire to drink their coffee and brandy. They would open the soiled pouch, which Gueret had fetched from his room, and spread out on the oilcloth the diamonds in all their elegant settings. Now and then Maria would absentmindedly put on an earring and then forget she had it on. Smiling, he would take it off her. The light from the stove lit up the devout expression on both their faces as they looked at the stolen jewels; they would then both sink into an almost psychopathic contemplation.

At the end of the week she said crossly that she could no longer keep their new clothes in her wardrobes, that moths would get at them, and that storing them meant losing the use of one whole room.

'What difference does that make?' he asked, unconcerned.

But she snapped at him. Gilbert had not yet found a suitable fence. That could take time, and he, Gueret, might be as glad as she would be to find a third lodger. Unless Gilbert succeeded in selling the little solitaire that she had taken to him to test the water . . . 'Then, pal,' she said, 'if that happens and we lay our hands on the money before the end of the winter, I guarantee we'll have a ball.'

But she refused to answer his questions.

Every morning after that, Gueret, perched on a rickety moped, went down to the plant. But he was no longer the tired, downtrodden yokel who kow-towed to that vile Mauchant; he had become a knight proud on his mechanical steed, a man with whom it was better not to pick a quarrel.

Little Nicole was the first to try.

On an outstandingly fine evening, Gueret had amused himself by riding back and forth across the desolate-looking field that had once struck gloom into his soul but where the dog now followed him, joyfully barking as it ran after him. Gueret breathed in deeply the air that was supposed to be so polluted, and gazed at the flatlands that he had once found so depressing. Now that he was going to leave them, he found they had a certain charm. It was not the jewels, nor the fortune that was yet to come, nor the new attitude of women towards him nor the sudden respect of men that made him happy. But he was happy. His looks were improving and every once in a while, seeing his reflection in a looking-glass, he was surprised to see how sun tanned he was; he admired his candid look and square shoulders and said to himself that Maria was really quite lucky after all.

On this particular evening, rather full of himself, he felt he was God's gift to someone. He went home to his boarding-house with well-defined amorous intentions – especially since it was Friday evening and the doting grandfather had gone back to his babe-in-arms.

Maria was not in the kitchen; it took him three minutes to locate her in the garden. She was wearing her black apron and scarf and looking down with a jaundiced air at her pitiful flower bed. Gueret gazed at her for a moment before calling out to her, surprised and a little troubled at desiring this woman whose mind was so obviously far removed from anything to do with love. He tiptoed soundlessly towards her and suddenly put his arms around her. She started, turned, and with incredible speed brandished the pruning knife she had been clutching in her right hand. Then she recognized Gueret, who, frightened and embarrassed, backed off.

'Don't ever do that again,' she said. '*Never*. I hate being taken by surprise.'

'But it's me,' he said shamefaced. 'You can't be afraid of me?'

She started to laugh. 'How could I be afraid of you? A nice young man who attacks only old jewellers!'

Gueret scowled. Sometimes he felt like telling her everything, admitting that it wasn't he. Now that they had shared a bed, plans; now that they had laughed together and together faced impudent salesmen and stuck-up waiters, he was under the impression – no, it was more than an impression – he felt they were bound by more interesting, warmer ties than shared guilt. And anyway, she ought to be reassured by Gueret's promise that once the jewels were sold they would both be rich – separately or together. No longer would she run the risk of seeing him arrested at dawn. And even if she did not really love him – and she often told him just that – she must nonetheless feel some affection for him.

Gueret had had a moral upbringing, and a small voice within reproved him for allowing himself to be loved for an evil deed. Nevertheless, each time he decided to tell her everything, he would back away, his tongue stilled by dire forebodings. It would be better to speak to her later, when they were in Senegal, or elsewhere, alone, transplanted to a new country; solitude would oblige them to stick together. In any event, at present he knew that his own fate was bound to hers. This was one of the reasons he desired her: he wanted to tame her physically. The other was more basic: accustomed to the women who worked at Samson's or, during his military service, to prostitutes, Gueret had never known love, physical love, never really discovered his own sensuality until he'd slept with this older woman. She might have tired of lovemaking, but in her gestures there was an experience, an abandon that made Gueret feel that before he had met her he had been a virgin. He took her in his arms, but she pushed him away with her grubby hands.

'What's got into you?' she asked. 'You're all worked up. Do you read porno magazines in the book-keeping department these days?'

He bridled. He said to himself that he was handsome, that she was no longer what is known as a pretty woman, she must be more frustrated physically than he was. After all, his desiring her at all was pretty flattering, he thought stupidly, refusing to believe what she had repeated obstinately from the start, that she was no longer interested in lovemaking. This indifference did not accord with her nocturnal activities, and Gueret was too green in matters of love to think that experience alone could have imparted the skills and sighs of a fulfilled woman.

'Well then, are you coming?' he asked. 'Don't you want to?'

She looked at him closely, with an expression of exasperation mingled, in spite of herself, with satisfied vanity. 'Tell me, Gueret,' she jeered, 'aren't you just a wee bit depraved? How can you find me sexy like this?' and she held out her hands, pointed to her wrinkles, her shapeless form, the grey in her hair. 'Don't you think you ought to try to find a woman your own age, someone a little fresher? What are you, near-sighted?'

'I like *you* as *you* are,' he said, accenting the 'you' and taking hold of her with a firm, virile hand, the way he knew women liked, at least in the movies. But she was not joking and she pushed him away before going back into the house.

'Come on, come on,' he said, following her into the house. 'I'm your lover, I've got every right – '

'You've got no right at all,' she said. 'I've already told you I'm not interested in that anymore. I like sleeping alone in my bed, stretched out across it, taking up the whole thing. I'm through with guys snoring by my side guys trying to prove themselves. And anyway, you have to force yourself.'

'I do?' Gueret said, flabbergasted. 'Not at all. Why do you say that?'

'Men have a thing about establishing their virility, they do it at the office, or with women or horses, or football . . . They always have to prove it somewhere or other. But it's not with women that you're going to prove it.'

'With what, then?' he asked, disgruntled, but intrigued in spite of himself, because after all she was speaking about him, about his character, and it was the first time anyone had taken any interest in him as a person, and not as a book-keeper or prospective husband. She was more interested in what he was than in what he did, and Gueret found this intoxicating.

'You've proved your manhood in other ways — by force, being a criminal. The rest is less important. Real gangsters — and I know a few in Marseilles — don't pay any attention to women, and if they do it's only later, after the essentials are taken care of.'

'But I'm not a gangster,' he said, irritated. 'I'm a twenty-seven-year-old guy who wants to sleep with a woman. You.'

'Well, I don't want to.' She turned her back on him, lit the stove. There was no hint of provocativeness in her tone; she really didn't want him. The reflection of the handsome young man he had seen in the mirror that very morning suddenly struck him as ridiculous and false.

'So it's all over between us.' To his surprise, he felt his voice shaking, just like that of a vapid young television star.

'It isn't over,' she said in the same weary voice as before, 'it never started. That's all. Now and again, yes, if you want, but not tonight.

'Maybe next year I'll be the one to beg you,' she went on, seeing his disappointed look. When he didn't smile, she suddenly lost her temper. 'Go see your friend Nicole and leave me in peace tonight! Not only do I feel like sleeping alone tonight, I feel like having dinner alone and being alone in this dump for once. Do you understand?'

Yes, he did understand. He understood that he must never ask for anything; he had to accept the crumbs that were thrown him or go away. Well, he would pull out; he'd show her.

'All right, I'm going to see Nicole,' he said with spurious enthusiasm. 'At least she doesn't spend the evening gardening and she think's I'm pretty hot stuff, and the boss's secretary does, too. So if you're not interested, too bad, or so much the better.'

Turning up his coat collar, he went off on his moped, followed by the jeering laughter his last statement had provoked.

Later that night he was in Nicole's room, in her rumpled bed. She was in the adjacent bathroom, singing a popular tune, and the stupid words of the song put the finishing touches to Gueret's depression. She came back into the room and stretched out on the bed, next to him. Her bathrobe was an unattractive pink, he thought, but still he smiled at her.

'It's been a long time, you know,' she said. 'I thought you'd forgotten me. Do you realize it's been two weeks?'

He shook his head seriously as he contemplated her.

She was pink and fresh-looking, she had a pretty, soft, supple body, the body of a modern young woman. She loved 'doing it' and had shrieked with pleasure a little while ago; he wondered why the hour that had just gone by had seemed so dull to him. She took up a hand-mirror from her night-table, held it in front of their faces, and looked at herself lying beside him. She leaned her head dreamily against his.

'We're pretty cute, don't you think?'

'Yes, yes, yes, we're very cute. I'd even say we're a cute couple,' he said derisively, noticing for the first time the flowered cretonne curtains, the large photograph of Robert Redford on the fake mantelpiece, the little dressing-table made of pseudo-mahogany, and, in front of it, a stool upholstered in terry cloth.

It was a nicely furnished room, Gueret thought, and oddly elegant for an employee as badly paid as she was. Furthermore, it was dazzlingly clean. In short, except for the long-skirted, idiotic doll sprawled on the chair, it was a pretty setting for Nicole.

Suddenly he saw again in his mind's eyes Maria's cold, gloomy room with its faintly soiled walls and the rickety table on which he would fling his clothes in a heap – either there, or on the fraying wicker garden-chair that looked dingy even outside in the summer and that simply did not belong in a room doomed to perpetual winter. Maria's room doubled as a tool shed – with its broken rakes, pruning knives, packets of seeds tossed into a corner. It was an ugly, desolate, barely lived-in room, but Gueret had seen it open up, spin, shrink, expand in the night. It would become a place of refuge or of perdition, depending upon Maria's deep silences or calm whispering, when her husky voice ushered in the heights of eroticism.

His face must have betrayed his longing because, with a frown, Nicole turned towards him. 'What's the matter? You don't like it here or you don't like it anymore?'

'Of course I do,' he replied weakly, 'of course I like it, I wouldn't be here otherwise. Now I must go,' he went on, not realizing the unfortunate sequence of his remarks as he firmly put both feet on the floor.

He suddenly felt the need to get out quickly. He could no longer stand this young woman with her cheerful room, her repellent doll, her ridiculous words of love. For two hours he had put up with her girlish antics. After all she was twenty-two, not twelve. But all at once she looked older. She sat up straight in bed, her features for once rigid with anger. He noted this and felt embarrassed by his detachment.

'Where are you going? You're bored, áren't you? Or are you going to see someone else?'

'Who? Me?' replied Gueret, trying to laugh scornfully. 'Me? You think I have time to chase after girls?'

'No!' Nicole replied, suddenly scarlet-faced. 'No, I don't think you've got time to chase after girls.'

Surprised, he looked at her. Anger suited her; her open bathrobe revealed a little breast, a clear, rosy skin. How could he prefer Maria to this beautiful girl? Maria was right: he really must be a pervert. For a fleeting moment he was ashamed of himself, but this sense of shame was so tenuous, so remote, that he almost had to force himself to feel it.

'What do you mean?' he asked as he struggled to tie his shoelaces. They had broken and been knotted so many times they no longer fitted through the eyelets. (He'd have to remember to buy new laces; there really wasn't much point in having two women: only one of them could be trusted to remember to buy laces, and that was Nicole; he couldn't imagine the other one doing it.)

Gueret got up. He would go home on his moped, stop in front of a neighbour's house so as not to make any noise, tiptoe up to her room . . . and then, once he was lying on top of her, she would have a hard time getting rid of him . . . She might not even want to. What was Nicole saying?

'I mean that it's not girls you're especially interested in now. They say you like them old, that's what they say.'

'What do you mean?' He already knew, of course. He ought to have looked indignant, to deny everything, but he was too busy dressing as quickly as possible, anxious to get out before she asked too direct a question, before she told him things about Maria he didn't want to hear. But like a judge, sitting calmly in her bed with arms crossed, she beat him to the draw.

'Your landlady, Madame Biron – what's this about some great thing between you? It's hard to believe.'

'What? Who told you that?' he asked, the astonishment in his voice already sounding hollow even to himself. 'That's ridiculous.'

'Yes, it's ridiculous, but everyone says it and not everyone is ridiculous. At first I didn't believe it. I said to myself that the idea of you and that old slut was too much. I was just telling Muriel, I said "Muriel, he's not really going to fall for that old whore from Marseilles, not that old soak?"'

It was the word 'soak' rather than 'old' that shocked

Gueret. Maria herself commented often enough on how old she was, and she rather enjoyed putting on the loving-mother act in public. The difference in age meant nothing to Gueret, especially not erotically. No, what shocked him was that Nicole could speak of Maria – authoritative, clearheaded Maria – as though she were a lush mooching around like a derelict in the back alleys of a port.

Nicole's indignation and sincerity were so strong that the only way he could think of defending his mistress against them was to admit that indeed they were lovers. But Maria had been adamant on that score: he was to disavow their relationship, ignore any provocation, laugh off indiscreet teasing – in short, deny everything. At the time he had thought her request noble, even heroic. But now he was wondering whether she wasn't actually guarding her own reputation rather than his. Perhaps, after all, she was ashamed of him. Probably so, since she refused to share her bed and was denying him her body; all this must mean she was ashamed of their liaison. Of course, he was younger than she, and in better physical shape, but this advantage, this superiority, ceased to exist the moment it did not exist for her.

'But for God's sake, age and physique must count for something in life!' said Gueret to himself.

After all, Nicole was certainly pretty, and it wasn't because she bored the hell out of him, or because she didn't appeal to him anymore, that everything and everybody else in the world was wrong – all the newspapers, films, public opinion polls, committees, whatever. Everyone said it over and over again: that in today's world it was the young, the handsome, charming, suntanned affluent young, who were the leaders, the winners. They were the cream of society. It certainly wasn't that dowdy, taciturn, hard-bitten fifty-year-old woman. And he was thunderstruck by this further revelation: that public opinion polls meant nothing to him. General approval did not alter facts, after all. Statistics could not prevent Maria from being the one who made him laugh, the one who aroused him.

'What do you have against Madame Biron?' he asked in a thick voice. He had finished struggling with his shoelaces and was edging towards his jacket and the door.

Nicole crowed: 'Your Madame Biron came to Carvin before you did! And there were quite a few guys at the plant and other places who knew your Madame Biron and didn't call her "Madame". She's not exactly untouched by human hands, if you know what I mean. Now those guys have become more choosy. They like women younger than her. But then, of course, I'm talking about normal guys.'

Gueret's voice, laden with an incomprehensible rage, lashed out in the ensuing silence.

'Christ! What's all this talk about being young?' he shouted. Nicole, astounded and a little frightened, just stared at him. He was exasperated, white with fury. He sensed only too well that if he had left Maria's bed satisfied he could have carried this whole thing off – that he could have bad-mouthed her and disowned her. But now that she had rejected him, he felt compelled to defend her.

'What's so great about being young?' he continued in a quieter tone while, with trembling fingers, he buttoned his jacket. 'What difference do you think it makes to me that you're young? I don't think that's exciting. It's only old people who find young flesh exciting. Didn't you know that?'

It flashed through Gueret's mind that with her mouth open Nicole looked like a chicken, and then he stopped seeing her. He had to go and see if there was any basis for the outlandish idea that he had just had about Maria, about himself, about the world in general. He had to go and see for himself if Maria really was all that different from others: uninterested in anything to do with present-day morality, fashion, convention – in short, with all contemporary guidelines. Yes, he simply had to go and see if she honestly didn't give a damn. He suddenly came to a decision, got up, grabbed Nicole by the wrist, and pushed her towards her clothes.

'You'll see if Madame Biron gets in my way! Tonight we'll sleep at my place for a change – and tomorrow I'll tell my old mistress to bring us breakfast in bed. How about that? Will that be enough for you?' He was already running down the stairs as Nicole hurriedly started to dress, but in spite of herself she slowed down gradually. With a victorious air he mounted his moped; she clung to his back, bent forward in a supplicating, frightened posture which was like a symbol of her innermost self but which Gueret could not see. It was a moonlit night, and they zigzagged under the moon, in and out of the slag heaps as if in broad daylight. Just before reaching the boarding-house, Gueret surprised himself by slowing down. Then suddenly he revved up again, nearly dumping Nicole. He spoke loudly as he pushed her up the stairs in front of him and, having slammed the front door, directed her in a loud voice: 'Straight up, first door on the right. Do you like it, darling?' He went on in a tone that was supposed to be lustful but that apparently did not ring true, since, once inside the room, Nicole remained motionless, her toes turned in, and obviously much embarrassed. She looked at the pictures of the Caribbean that hung on the walls and said in a low, genteel voice, 'What's all that? Do you want to go there?'

'I'd like to,' Gueret whispered back. 'Yes, I'd like that,' he repeated in a loud, unnatural voice, like some ham actor in a B film. 'If you want, I'll take you with me. We'll live in the sun.'

Nicole was smiling. Her fright gone, she entered into the spirit of the thing. 'What a good idea, darling!' she cried out in a piercing theatrical tone. 'What fun it would be! What would we do, besides make love?' she asked, looking towards the wall and speaking in a voice she thought sexy, but which struck Gueret as grotesque.

The whole situation was indeed grotesque, with Nicole tiptoeing and speaking without looking at him, her head turned towards the wall that was the source of his bad humour, worry, and unease.

'Well, why don't we go to bed?' he went on in the same silly tone. 'Come here!'

Unthinkingly she did as she was told and sat down on the bed, close to Gueret, who looked at her and suddenly did not know what to do next. How on earth could he take this dull little biddy in his arms? How could he possibly arouse any passion in her, make her moan with pleasure, when a couple of yards beyond, on the other side of the partition, Maria might be listening? No, of course she wasn't listening – but still she was sure to hear, and that was frightening to contemplate.

Nicole, for her part, gazed at him with frightened docility and humility. He was beginning to look like a fool, he thought furiously. And that bitch Maria was making him impotent! That was the last straw.

'Should I take my clothes off?'

Helplessly Gueret looked at her as though she had uttered an obscenity. Nicole blushed. He tried to pull himself together. With a last effort, he articulated carefully, 'Oh, yes! I'd love to see you in the nude. Kiss me!'

His tone was so insincere that Nicole didn't budge, but still as if they were in a bad film, she waited a moment, then with a ridiculous whinny, but without enthusiasm, began, 'Oh, my darling, but – '

Just then the door opened wide and banged against the wall. On the threshold, looking immensely tall to both of them, loomed Maria in a shabby dressing-gown, her hair dishevelled, her dark eyes dull.

'Well?' she said.

Nicole automatically got off the bed, bowed her head, and in honeyed tones muttered an incongruous 'Good evening, madame', as she backed away. But Maria cut short her civilities.

'Do you think this is a bordello?' she asked Gueret in a flat voice. 'If so, go to the field across the way for your fun and games. You'll find plenty of room there and I'll be able to get some sleep. Now get out!'

'But,' stammered Gueret, 'this is my room.'

'Oh no, it isn't!' Maria quickly rejoined, stamping her heel on the floor to emphasize her point. 'No, this is *my* room. It's a room that I rent out, quite cheap, if you want to know, to boarders – to single men only. On the other hand, outside it's free, completely free. You've got three minutes to get the hell out of here. I need my sleep.'

She closed the door behind her without even slamming it, thus putting the finishing touch to Gueret's humiliation.

'Who does she think she is? Who?' he kept repeating, staggering as if he'd just received a physical blow.

But Nicole was already tugging at his sleeve and whining, 'Come on, let's go.'

They got back on the moped and returned to Nicole's place under an impersonal moon that had lost its brightness just as it was about to disappear under the horizon. Once they were back, Nicole didn't even bother to listen to Gueret's garbled explanations. She was shivering with cold and possibly delayed reaction. Her head was bowed, and as she turned towards her door, Gueret saw her back: it betrayed something his had also betrayed more than once, but Maria's never: humiliation.

'You saw, didn't you? So you did see how it is?' he asked.

'Yes, I saw.'

'You still think she's my mistress?' he shouted after her retreating back. She did not answer or even turn around.

Alone this time, Gueret went back at top speed to find Maria. He was going to insult her, beat her, maybe rape her. She would be forced to see what an angry man was like. He did a few miles as fast as his engine would go so he could sustain his mood. But when he got back, the night had gone and so had Maria. The house was empty. For a split second Gueret was delighted by the crazy thought that she was jealous, but quickly he succumbed to the worry that she might not come back to him.

She was gone for three days, and during those three days Gueret reverted to his former pitiful self: his step slowed, his head was bowed, his voice low-pitched. His tie was once more knotted tightly and he stopped hailing the dog. Nicole barely spoke to him. Mauchant, reassured, was worse than ever, as Gueret shuffled about.

It was only on the second day that it occurred to him to check on the jewels. They were still there; he laughed nervously as he realized how little he cared. He clung to the remedies of the poor-spirited. He carefully watered Maria's plants and vegetables, but he slept badly. Physically he let himself go. For three days, except for tightening his tie, almost to the point of strangulation, he did not change his clothes, putting on the same shirt, trousers, and increasingly rumpled jacket.

At about four o'clock on the last day, Mauchant, at the high point of vengefulness, excoriated him for his messy appearance. Gueret, beaten down and silent, let his glance wander to the slag heaps.

'Tell me,' said Mauchant, echoing Maria's words, 'what do you think this is, a bordello?'

Considering that he had set foot in one just once in his life, it was the final touch to be treated as though he were an habitué.

'Can't you do something about your clothes? This isn't a pigsty. Or maybe you don't own any other jacket. Your wardrobe . . .'

Mauchant stopped. Something in the way Gueret was standing alerted him. The fool had straightened up, stiffened, his look riveted on the slag heaps. Automatically Mauchant glanced at them, but he could see nothing except some white smoke issuing from a roof beyond them, on the left. And he did not understand why Gueret stood up with a suddenly delighted air that was once more authoritative, shoved him aside unceremoniously as though he were a mere object, and dashed to the door.

'Gueret!' howled Mauchant. 'Gueret, come back!'

'Go to hell!' replied Gueret without even looking back at his tormentor, who had once more become powerless. And when Mauchant leaned out the window to hurl insults at him, Gueret's bike was already flying towards the white smoke.

Maria had been to the hairdresser's and she was wearing a new coat and light make-up, all of which Gueret noticed only later. As soon as he arrived he dropped his precious machine, crossed the kitchen in two strides, and without looking at her took Maria in his arms. He acted with such firmness that she didn't put up a struggle. His cheek rested on her hair and, not stirring, he listened to the thumping of his heart against that of this bitch – this bitch who had kept him awake, who had obsessed him for three days and three nights. There was no thought of giving her hell, beating her up, even questioning her; she had come home, she was not fighting him. All was well. His heartbeat slowed down and he let out a small sigh of contentment.

'Was I scared!' he said.

Quiet but docile, she moved a little against him, without looking up. 'Scared of what?' she asked.

Her voice was muffled in Gueret's jacket; he held her so tight that she couldn't see him. Thus he was able to speak and she to hear without either of them laughing.

'Well, I thought you were going to turn me in,' he said with a smile.

On the following Saturday, while riding in a bus to Lille, Maria refused to answer Gueret's questions. Sitting back in her seat, her hands crossed on her bag, wearing her worn black coat, she looked just like a peasant woman going to town with her son. As soon as they left the bus she hailed a cab – unaccustomed luxury – with so natural a gesture that Gueret was awed.

'Twenty-three Rue des Hongrois,' she said as she slipped into the back seat.

'What in God's name are we going to do there?' whispered Gueret.

'You'll see.' Looking exasperated, she shut her eyes, but she couldn't help smiling.

Twenty-three Rue des Hongrois was an old stone house in an elegant section of Lille. It had an impressive entrance, with a coat of arms emblazoned above the door and a large paved courtyard with a small door, which Maria opened. She switched on the light as she entered and immediately went to the back of the room, where she opened a window. Gueret found himself in an opulent-looking living-room furnished in loud bad taste, half Art Deco, half colonial style: a sofa upholstered in black leather, metal lamps that had once been modern, oblong mirrors, and two Moroccan-style pouffes. The effect was pretentious and very ugly, but it struck Gueret as it had Maria: as being the epitome of luxury. She had turned around, and her look, which had been anxious, quickly became triumphant when she saw the blissful, dazzled expression on Gueret's face.

'Well, what do you think of it? We're now tenants, pal.' She waved a key.

'Pretty snappy,' replied Gueret, standing still on the wine-coloured wall-to-wall carpet.

'Come on, sit down! That's Russian leather, but it's meant to be sat on,' she said, pointing to the sofa.

Gueret sat down carefully, stretched out his legs, and in a swift movement put his feet on the Russian leather. With a cigarette dangling from the corner of his mouth, looking cynical, he leered at Maria and said in a lordly manner, 'Not too shabby, sweetheart. How about a drop of port and some potato chips?'

Maria seldom acknowledged Gueret's jokes, but this time she fell right in with his mood and answered with a curtsy, 'I'll get it; don't move.'

She went out, slammed a few doors, then returned with a glass in her hand.

'Here you are; it's vermouth, I forgot about port, but you'll have some next Saturday.'

'Next Saturday? How long did you rent this place for?'

'Six months. That'll give Gilbert time to sell the rest. But you haven't seen anything yet. Come on.'

Gueret followed her to a tiny garden that had been freshly dug over, then to a bedroom that had been made up. It contained a huge bed covered with a bedspread made of black satin woven with gold thread, two oriental lamps on rosewood bedside tables, and a chrome dressing-table in the mirror of which was reflected an equally gleaming bathroom. Startled and dazzled, Gueret looked around.

'You'll see the other room later,' she said, 'but first try this.' She opened a cupboard from which she took something dark that she tossed into his arms. 'It's a tuxedo,' she said. 'I also bought myself a dress. We talked about living it up, didn't we? Well, we're starting tonight. Later we'll come back here to *our* apartment. Tomorrow morning we'll sleep in; and in the evening we'll return to the Wisteria. Does that suit you?' Her voice was low, controlled, but her eyes shone with pleasure and pride. Something childlike about her had come out.

'Does it suit me? Are you kidding?' replied Gueret. 'How you do go on!' He was holding up the tuxedo as he looked in a mirror, lifting his chin and thrusting out his chest. 'Does it suit me! Mauchant can bray all week if he wants, I'll be thinking about this place.'

Maria stirred. The continuing Mauchant-Gueret

hostilities exasperated her. She was constantly surprised that Gueret had not yet murdered him in some dark corner of the plant. To change the subject, Gueret took off his jacket and donned the tuxedo. 'We'll paint the town red, the two of us. Look out, Lille, here we come!'

And indeed, a few hours later, in Lille, things were buzzing. Maria and Gueret were in a nightclub decorated in a style similar to that of their apartment. Maria, her hair now somewhat dishevelled, was singing 'Melancholy', a popular tune from the 1940s, while Gueret, a shade tipsy and in high spirits, clung to a hostess. Maria's singing aroused some laughter, and some sympathy. Gueret, who had clapped loudly, tried to drag her onto the dance floor, but she resisted. She had joined forces with the bandleader and the two of them reminisced about old hits, songs entitled 'Gypsy', 'Sentimental Journey', 'Stardust': tunes unfamiliar to Gueret, who found himself dancing once more with the hostess.

'The singer's your mother, or what?' she asked.

'My aunt,' he replied through clenched teeth. This was his version of Maria's instructions: the word 'aunt' held more romantic overtones than 'mother'.

'At your age you go out with an aunt?'

Gueret shrugged his shoulders. 'She's got her points.'

'So tell me. What kind of points? I hope they're not unmentionable . . .' The girl was sarcastic and aggressive. She had had too much to drink, and Gueret was irritated by her sneering tone.

'So what's this about your aunt anyway? And first of all, Aunt what?'

'Maria,' he replied without thinking. 'Actually, Marianne,' he went on.

Although there was no real need for it, they had decided to adopt aliases. Who, in their circumscribed lives, would recognize them in this provincial town with its closed society? And who, in this sleazy nightclub, could possibly know them? But Maria had wanted his name to be Raoul, a name he thought lacked class. He would have preferred a romantic name – something like 'François-Xavier' or 'Sébastien'. But Marie had said no, on account of the initials, so now he was 'Raoul' instead of 'Roger'. In any case, it had been twenty years, since his mother's death, that anyone had even called him 'Roger'. He was Gueret to everybody except Nicole, who called him 'my pet', 'my darling', 'honey', and other silly names; Maria didn't call him anything.

'Well?' The woman had stopped dancing; she really reeked of booze. 'Come on, out with it! What's so great about your Aunt Marianne? What are her good points? Want me to ask her?'

'No,' he replied, vaguely uneasy. 'No, I told you, it's just that she's funny . . . she makes me laugh, that's all.'

The woman stared at him, disbelieving. She smiled suddenly and let fall a torrent of inanities. Gradually her voice grew louder and the dancers around them stopped, curious.

'Well, well, well, she makes you laugh, does she? Ha! That takes the cake! With her sad songs, her droopy look, her taffeta dresses? That makes you laugh? Aunt Marianne makes you laugh? It couldn't be because you're sweet Auntie's gigolo, could it?'

To top things off, just then the music stopped and

Gueret found himself in the middle of the dance floor, surrounded by smirking dancers. He looked for Maria but couldn't see her, and started to panic. In an effort to seem relaxed, he tried putting his hands in his pockets, but he couldn't insert them into the tuxedo, which was too tight; finally, he put them behind his back. The girl was completely hysterical.

'You know, he's damn funny, our pretty boy,' she said loudly. 'Would you believe every night he trails behind Auntie, the singer of sad songs – now, that's the sort of thing that goes on in the sticks. He may be thirty, but still he takes Auntie out to paint the town red. Some set-up, huh?'

Gueret's face was flushed. He signalled to Maria, whom he'd finally spotted – but so had the girl.

'Little country boy's blushing – delicate, isn't he? Oh so sensitive. Well, where's Auntie?'

'Here I am,' said Maria in a calm voice. Brushing aside the smirking couples, she took a step towards the girl, who edged back.

'I told you Auntie was here!'

'Do you mind?' Maria spoke quietly, but her hissing, dangerous voice stopped the girl for a moment. She might have stopped for good had not a lightly tanned man in dark glasses, followed by a brawny character wearing a pea-green checked jacket, stopped behind them.

'Well,' said the man in glasses, 'are they bothering you, my pretty?' He had put an arm around the girl's neck and pretended not to see Gueret who, finally breaking his silence, tried to smooth things over.

'It's all a mistake,' he said. 'This lady was only joking;

it was a misunderstanding, there's nothing to worry about.' He tried to smile, but he was worried; he didn't like the look of the two thugs, who were obviously troublemakers. This evening on the town was beginning to turn sour; he had had too much to drink to think clearly, and this place was set up differently from the Three Ships.

'Come on, Maria, let's get out of here. It's getting late.'

She didn't answer; she was looking at the man with glasses.

'You'll have to apologize before leaving,' he said, blowing cigarette smoke into Gueret's eyes. Gueret moved his head back. Someone behind them started to laugh and Maria took a step towards the joker, who also involuntarily backed away. The crowd had suddenly stopped laughing, and now it was curiosity rather than jeering that prevailed.

'Hey, you backcountry gangster,' Maria said in the same level voice she had used before, 'how about minding your own goddamn business? You chorus-line thugs don't amuse me. Let me tell you something: I've seen real gangsters in Marseilles, big-time hoodlums. First they leave the customers alone. Next, they're polite to women; next, they never wear dirty shirts, their nails aren't filthy, and they don't wear their hair in spit curls. You follow me? So get out of my way. My nephew and I'll come back in a few years to see if you've cleaned up your act. Get out of my way, big boy.'

The man had unsuccessfully tried to interrupt her; he was livid. The crowd was now snickering at him. He automatically backed away as he caught Maria's gimlet eye, but as soon as her back was turned he jumped on Gueret, who had delayed too long before following her.

'Good for a laugh, is it?' As he spoke he kicked Gueret in

the knee and punched him in the stomach. Gueret, stunned, doubled up, received a kick in the ribs and rolled on the floor. The man had lost all control. He kept kicking Gueret towards the door. Gueret, blinded, his nose bloodied, tried clumsily to defend himself. At the entrance he rolled over; the small-time pimp, with the help of a doorman, threw him out and closed the door.

Gueret found himself at Maria's feet. She stood there, in the dawn light, on the purple pavement, and looked down with an expression that was not compassion. His ribs hurt, his nose was bleeding, and he felt nauseated. He leaned against the door and tried to get up.

'Well?'

Gueret fell back, put his hand in front of his face, looked at the blood on his fingers, and wiped them on his trousers. He threw back his head, eyes closed, and breathed deeply. The sounds of a tango reached them. 'It smells nice,' he said suddenly, 'it smells of the country.'

'You don't mind having the hell beaten out of you?' Maria was still standing, motionless, like a judge. Gueret felt far removed from her, from the brawl, from everything.

'No,' he said quietly, 'no, it's not important.'

'What *is* important?' Maria's harsh voice was almost devoid of expression.

'What is important is that it's nice out here at this hour. The music's good. This empty street is beautiful. We'll go back to our pretty house, sleep together – that's what's important.' He spoke gently, in a manly, confident voice, and the woman facing him knelt down to look at him closely. Her fury had become a passionate interrogation.

'I can't help it,' she said, 'I have to be able to respect a man. I want someone free who can say "shit", to thugs, to honest guys and will say it to gangsters; a man who's respected, do you understand?'

'Would you feel better if I had killed him?' asked Gueret gently. 'You're angry, aren't you?'

'Yes. I'm ashamed.'

His head had fallen to one side. He did not look at her. A lock of hair had fallen over one eye. He looked wounded, indifferent. For the first time she thought him handsome.

He spoke slowly. 'People don't respect me; they never have – not at school, or at home, or at the plant. People have always treated me badly and still do.'

Maria was leaning over him. She had taken his chin in her hand and was trying to pull his face towards her so that she could look him in the eye, but he resisted; he had spoken without looking at her.

She said, 'Yes, but one evening you did rebel, didn't you? You said "shit" to everybody, to the plant, the slag heaps, the law. You killed someone. At least you did that once.'

'You think so?'

He was suddenly lost in thought and she got up, out of breath, exhausted. She felt as though they had said things to each other that they ought not to have said, and she was under the impression she had not had the last word. She had progressed from scorn and anger with him, even fury, to an ambiguous feeling that was unlike anything she had ever experienced before.

'Are you coming?' she said harshly, to reassure herself.

Gueret was now on his feet, and carefully dusted off

his sleeve. 'There's a stain; what a drag.' He seemed more perturbed by his stained tuxedo than by having been beaten up in front of his mistress.

Another wave of fury swept over her. 'Are you coming? You can play the lady-killer somewhere else.'

He looked at her and smiled, then said: 'No, no; there's something I've got to do.' He turned towards the door, opened it, and disappeared into the dive before she had a chance to realize what he was up to. She remained alone at the door, resisting an ill-defined notion of also going in, of following him. Then she leaned against the dark doorway, which was turning grey in the early morning light. She breathed deeply to calm something inside her that was bothering her, and noticed with surprise that it did indeed smell nice outside.

Gueret stopped for a moment in the shadows, a little way from the bar, his legs somewhat unsteady. No one had seen him come in. He could hear his adversaries, elbows resting on the bar, speaking in angry voices. The muscleman sounded ironic, and the sadist, the would-be gangster, was getting irritated.

'You didn't have to kick him,' the strong man said. 'You saw he didn't know how to fight. You fight dirty when you're annoyed.'

'What makes you think I'm annoyed?'

The man, whom Gueret now thought of as 'a chorus-line thug', had a high voice. Maria was right to talk about spit curls. She really knows how to describe things, thought Gueret, as he shook with silent laughter. He wanted to laugh about everything. It was all funny. What the hell was he doing here with dried blood clogging his nose and his ribs aching, while those miserable characters at the bar talked about him as though they had nothing else to do at this hour? He had become the focus of interest, he thought derisively, and a feeling of superiority, quite out of keeping for a man who had just been beaten up, swept over him. He was going to have his face pushed in again; at the prospect, he sucked in his guts where it still hurt. For once he did not stop to ask himself what he was going to do, or why, or what people would say. He was simply going to do what he wanted to do. He felt free; it was a vibrant, intoxicating feeling, one of bliss, of tranquillity. He recognized the sense of freedom although he had never before experienced it. Funny, he thought, that his particular brand of freedom consisted in getting himself kicked. He moved into the light.

The woman, the tart, was the first to notice him. She emitted a clucking sound that made the others turn around. People sitting at the tables did not see them. Seated on stools at the bar were the bouncer, the strong man, and the sadist, as well as the woman. No one else: a relief to Gueret. Throughout that ridiculous brawl he had been more afraid of the frightened anonymous faces of the customers than he had been of the more precisely delineated ones of his three antagonists.

'I'll be damned,' said the doorman, 'he's come back for more?' He got off his stool as he spoke; so did the small-time thug; the strong man, still sitting at the bar, turned to look at Gueret, with a shade of sympathy, it seemed to him.

'What are you doing here, buddy? You ought to be in bed. You're all bashed up.'

Gueret had stopped three feet away. He looked at them with what they took to be indecision. The sadist, taken aback for a moment, swaggered again.

'Leave him be. If he's looking for trouble, I'll see he gets it. Excuse me a minute – I wouldn't want to mess up my clothes.' He threw off his jacket and with a nervous gesture threw it to the woman, who, either absentminded or fascinated by Gueret, dropped it. He started to insult Gueret, but deciding there wasn't time for that, took up a boxer's stance, leading with his left, his right protecting his face. Just like a film, Gueret thought, as he balanced lightly on his feet, his arms hanging down. He felt miles away and relaxed, oh so relaxed.

'This time it's your own show, without me,' said the strong man. 'I warn you, Stéphane, this time you're on your own.'

'And you'll get no assistance from me,' said the bouncer.

They seemed aloof, disgusted. The man named Stéphane shot them a look that was at first incredulous, then furious.

'I don't need you. Come on, you dirty asshole, are you ready?'

'Here I am,' said Gueret tamely. He took two steps forward, stopped a right punch on his right side, a left hook to his cheek, but this did not stop him and he caught the other by the throat. In his hands he held something squirming, wrapped up in silky cloth. A 'dirty shirt', he vaguely remembered as he closed his eyes while he took a volley of blows all over his body. He was surprised that they didn't hurt. He felt the impact but not the pain. Anyway, he was so close to his opponent and clutched him so hard that the blows were growing weaker, less well aimed. He tightened his grip without conviction, slowly, so as to keep the object that was squirming and looking more and more revolting from escaping him. The fight seemed to be going on and on. He was getting bored now that the blows had almost stopped. He heard sharp voices. The others, in spite of their promises, were meddling. He was being pulled back; they were trying to take his opponent away from him. The woman was screaming. He was being furiously shaken. The sleeve of the strong man passed before his eyes while a rough hand gripped his own fingers, lifting them up one by one, and the dirty shirt was snatched from his grasp.

Gueret resisted; he could have resisted longer if the object he was holding so firmly hadn't suddenly become heavy, just as repellent in its limpness as it had been in its frenzy. All the time his face had been buried in something black and shiny that reeked of brilliantine: the top of the bully's head. When the latter had fallen, Gueret could see again. He blinked, aware finally of voices and the clamour that filled the bar and seemed to him absurd and melodramatic. Somebody had given him a shove, and he was leaning on the bar with another nosebleed. He watched people hover over something on the floor, something he was able to recognize, from the pointed and overly shiny shoes, as being the bully. They were the same shoes that had repeatedly kicked him a short while ago when he was lying in front of the door. The strong man apparently bore him no grudge even though he had savagely turned back Gueret's fingers and dragged him to the door. They had to step aside to let two unknown characters, who looked panicky, carry out his adversary by his arms and legs, head dangling. Gueret saw his throat as they went by: it bore an ugly red mark. He felt not the remotest twinge of unease as he wondered mildly if he had killed him.

They went through the open door. The morning air struck Gueret as being part of a dream that was just as unlikely as the whole evening had been. He also heard Maria asking, 'Is he dead?' Her voice held no overtones of fear or pleasure.

He heard the muscleman say, 'Go away now,' and Gueret massaged his fingers for a second, surprised to find them so numb.

He had been right a little while ago: there really was a smell of country in the air. He couldn't help pointing it out to Maria, whom he could see quite clearly now. She looked tired; her forehead was smooth and she looked a bit sulky in the morning light. For once she admitted that he was right and, when he insisted, even acknowledged that it smelled of new-mown hay.

He had fallen asleep as soon as he got into the bed under the embroidered damask spread. He hadn't even felt Maria loosen his shoes or take off his tuxedo. He woke up around eleven, his mouth all dried out, wondering at first where he was. Daylight filtered through the blinds. What first came into his line of vision was his tuxedo on a clothes hanger, swinging round and round like a body.

Maria's dress, with brown bloodstains on the dark fabric, lay on the floor. Gueret, his eyes open, torso naked, hands crossed under the nape of his neck, looked at the unfamiliar walls, amused by the scattered stained clothing – the jetsam of their evening together. He couldn't remember much, so he turned to the dark heap on the other side of the large bed to ask a few questions, but what he had mistaken for a sleeping Maria was a heap of crocheted blankets all bundled up in the dark corner. Worried, Gueret sat up, listened intently, and finally heard a muted radio playing in the next room. Reassured, he got up a little too quickly and groaned. They must have broken his bones the night before. Then he caught sight of himself in the large mirror on the wardrobe door. He was startled. Maria had left him his drawers to sleep in, but his torso and thighs were covered with black and blue bruises. Seen from the side, his nose and upper lip were red and swollen.

Some brawl, he thought and gave a small satisfied smile.

He looked into the living-room before entering it. Maria was sitting on the Russian leather sofa facing the french window, that opened on to the empty garden. She was smoking, her hand resting on the radio. She was motionless, her eyes mere slits. Gueret seldom saw her without her seeing him; he had caught her in a natural pose. Not that she ever put on airs; but now she wore a secret look, different from the one she normally presented to him. Her expression was sadder, more thoughtful, more detached. Gueret picked up his evening shirt from the bed and put it on; Maria had often laughed at his idiotic modesty.

After a bit of static, the radio emitted solemn and sentimental music, Sunday music, he thought, the sort that made him feel uneasy about going barefoot. Taken unawares, Maria started when she saw him, put her feet on the floor and stood up.

They looked at each other for a moment, then smiled

politely. He was embarrassed, he didn't quite know why, and for once she also seemed so. But embarrassed by what?

'You're awake now?' she asked. 'You're quite a mess. Come here; let's have a look.'

Gueret stood in front of her, as though for an inspection. She had opened his shirt and with an expert and impersonal hand felt his ribs, his leg muscles, his shoulder blades. Occasionally she whistled when she saw a bruise darker than the others. 'Does this hurt? Here?'

Blissfully he allowed himself to be felt. He loved having her take care of him in this way. He couldn't decide whether her gestures were those of a mother or a horse trader, but they were the gestures of a woman taking care of her man after a brawl. And when she dismissed him, patting his side quite familiarly this time, he sighed.

'The coffee's on,' she said. 'While you're about it, will you bring me a cup?'

In the chrome-plated alcove known as the kitchen Gueret, his hands shaking, poured out two cups. He noticed that his joints were swollen, and like a schoolboy he sucked his fingers. Then he remembered the reason for the swelling. The recollection made him tremble so violently that he had to put down the cups at once. Terrified, he leaned against the wall. He kept opening and closing his large hands and fingers that seemed not to belong to him, unable to remember whether or not the evening before he had held someone by the throat so tightly he had killed him. The man had been wrested from him; he remembered seeing his limp arms and legs as he was carried out by two men, his throat marked by a red line. Was he dead? Gueret couldn't remember anything clearly. Maria was the only one he could question, and he didn't dare. When you stab a man who hasn't done anything to you seventeen times, for money, you don't panic because you've half strangled or completely strangled a thug who tried to pick a quarrel. That didn't add up.

Weak at the knees, he went back into the living-room, put the cup in front of Maria, and to avoid her eyes went over to look down at the garden, or rather at the bit of ground that passed for such. The freshly turned plot must have measured about nine by six – 'the exact dimensions of a tomb,' he said to himself morbidly. He started talking loudly to Maria.

'You want to do some planting here, too? What will you choose? Sweet peas? I like sweet peas.'

She answered from where she was sitting, talking about exposure, humus, fertilizer, seedlings, while Gueret, hidden by the blinds, examined his hands, shirt, and arms, as though something in them might give him a clue about the crime he might have committed.

Maria's voice finally broke out above the din of the music. 'I listened to Radio Lille this morning, do you hear? Guess what? Except for a drug-store robbery and a grocery-store fire, the sleep of the good citizens of Lille was undisturbed. Imagine that – the night was uneventful. Do you hear? Answer me?'

Gueret closed his eyes with relief and took a moment to reply, absentmindedly. 'Yes, yes, things are under control in Lille.' Then, firmly: 'Yes, sweet peas would really be nice.'

She watched him as he crossed the room, and heard

him say cheerfully, 'I'm going to soak my black and blue bruises in the pink bathtub.' He then laughed immoderately at his flat joke.

She followed him with vaguely worried eyes.

The son of the director of
Samson's, Francis, who drove around in a convertible
and who wore cravats to work, had been requested by his
father to spend more time at the factory and less in Paris
nightclubs. One day, as he was crossing the courtyard,
the young dandy called out to Gueret in an unexpectedly
friendly tone, 'Well, Gueret, how are things going?'

Jonas, the young trainee, the one who was always delighted by Gueret's outbursts, had laughed at Gueret's
astonishment.

'Don't you know why Samson Junior's so friendly to
you? It's because of Mauchant.'

'Because of Mauchant?' Gueret was mystified. Despite the irregular life he had been leading for some weeks, the plant continued to be sovereign, unassailable; it represented Authority.

'Yes, because of Mauchant. You won't be surprised to learn he complained about you, but he blew it by choosing Samson Junior to complain to.' The young man blushed, looked down, and finally said in a whisper, 'Your landlady. He told him the woman's older than you and that you weren't normal. And he put his foot right in his mouth, because Samson Junior's got a mistress who's forty-five! And Mauchant had been hoping to step into Le Hideux's shoes when he retires. Boy, did he blow it!'

Although amused, Gueret did not for an instant consider telling Maria about these developments. Anything to do with the plant bored her. Not like her garden.

He was supposed to rush back every evening to help her cultivate the soil, but on this day she was already busy in the garden when he arrived. When she saw him, followed by the dog, she gave a vague gesture of greeting. He realized after a furtive look at her that it would be better to say nothing.

He had been digging for ten minutes when she called to him, 'Listen, I didn't tell you, I got a letter from Gilbert. In one month the guy from Marseilles will be here with the money.'

'Is that so?' said Gueret, straightening up and rubbing his back. 'In a month? Well,' he continued with a laugh, 'you're not going to enjoy your flowers for long.' He pointed to the seedlings at his feet. 'You won't have more than a week at most to enjoy them!'

She seemed absentminded and didn't answer.

'Why don't we stop?' he asked, encouraged by the silence. 'No point in all this. We can't take these flowers with us.'

She snapped at him, 'That's just what I like, things that are useless. No one's forcing you to do this, so if you think it's a drag . . .' She dug her spade in again, and Gueret, shrugging his shoulders, was going to do likewise when she turned to him. 'You're right. Flowers are full of passion. They know when they're not liked. You might kill them. Why not ride down to Gerrier's and get some wine? I forgot to get some.'

Relieved, Gueret put down the spade, protesting feebly, and without conviction, 'I don't see why I'd make your flowers die. They like me.'

'I wonder why?' she said sarcastically.

But he had already mounted his moped and was on the road. As he took the turn he nearly ran into Madame Rousseau on her bicycle. She was the only neighbour to whom Maria deigned to smile or speak.

As Gueret disappeared in the distance, the poor woman shrieked, sounded her horn furiously, braked, and skidded up to where Maria stood. As she got off, she said, 'What a turn your boarder gave me! My knees are still wobbly.'

'He's wild,' said Maria tersely.

Fat Madame Rousseau mopped her brow and bravely got back on her bike. 'He may be wild, but he's a nice boy. He looked after your flowers, morning and night, when you were away two weeks ago. I could see him, from my house, watering them. You can't say he's a bad boarder. Well, see you soon.'

She departed, leaving a stunned Maria spade in hand. She looked alternately in the directions one had gone and the other would return; she looked at Gueret's raincoat hanging on the gate, at the flowers. She slowly took her feet out of her heavy wooden shoes, removed the scarf from her head, and went back into the house.

She unhooked her apron as she went by and hung it on the corner of the mantelpiece, then from a cupboard took a glass and a bottle of dry vermouth, her favourite aperitif. Pensively she poured out one drink, then another. Glass in hand, she went to the stove and reluctantly, unseeingly stirred something in a pot with a wooden spoon. She looked along the wall to a cheap mirror hanging on a nail and caught sight of herself. She stiffened. Her features, which were perfectly still, wore a cold, hostile look. She dropped the spoon, raised her hand to her chin, then to her hair, which she fluffed out with a light gesture, but carelessly, without apparent interest. Opposite her, the face remained immobile, aloof; it was the face of pure boredom and indifference. The clear steady eyes, under their proud lids, looked more surprised than pained when round, heavy tears began to run down her expressionless face. She was still watching them flow when the sound of the moped reached her.

As Gueret came in carrying a wine crate, the dog at his heels, Maria was leaning as usual over the stove, her back to him. He put the wine down and called the dog back. Although the kitchen was forbidden territory, it had already put three paws forward and was poised at the edge of this tempting space.

'Stay!' Gueret said.

The dog looked expectantly at Maria, waiting for the

'Out!' and the gesture that always made the man grab its collar and expel it from paradise. But Maria said nothing, didn't utter the usual sounds, did not turn around, and, unable to resist, the dog put one paw forward, then another, and, half crouching, went through the kitchen and lay at Maria's feet. Its ears lay flat and its tail wagged wildly. Still not turning, Maria spoke to the dog. It was the first time she had done so, and Gueret noted it with delight.

'Well, you? A month ago you were in the street; a week ago you were in the garden; the other day you were in the hall – and today it's the kitchen! What a nerve!'

The dog whimpered and wagged its tail in sheer bliss. Maria leaned down and patted its head. Then she crouched down and the dog licked her face.

'You're fatter, your coat's soft, you look happy. Finding a master agrees with you.'

'It agrees with me, too,' said Gueret hesitantly. But Maria made no comment.

A little later, as they sat at the table under a swinging naked light bulb, Gueret said, putting his finger on a spot on the map of Africa spread in front of them, 'There, see? With ten willing guys, real workers, I'll set up the most beautiful lumberyard you ever saw. First I'll lower the prices, then I'll jack 'em up.'

'And I'll set up a huge bordello,' said Maria in an amused voice, 'with lots of white girls out front and a huge hothouse full of exotic flowers in the back.'

'And at night I'll come with my men to see the flowers and the women,' Gueret said with a smile. 'Of course, I'll only have eyes for one really.'

Sitting perfectly still, they both looked at the map; for once they were on the same wavelength. The dog, reacting to the atmosphere, had its head in Maria's lap and didn't stir. The window looking out on the wretched little garden was closed. Outside, despite the slag heaps, the air was redolent of summer. Gueret was in his shirt sleeves. Anyone looking at them through the window would have thought them a happy middle-class couple dreaming about the Club Méditerranée.

One idyllic week went by. The following weekend, Gueret, in the middle of the living-room of the apartment in Rue des Hongrois, in his tuxedo, which had been cleaned but the sleeves of which were still too short, was balancing on one foot and trying with some anguish, to button his starched collar. He was waiting for Maria, who, unlike her usual self, was taking forever in the bathroom – just like one of those fussy women she so little resembled. Gueret stood in front of the mirror adjusting his bow tie and decided he looked quite nice. But his enthusiasm gradually ebbed, and he was just smothering a yawn when the door opened.

'Look,' said Maria as she came in holding her left shoe in her hand, 'this sort of thing bores me. These clodhoppers are killing me. D'you mind?'

She sat down, took off her other shoe, and vigorously massaged her feet. She looked cheerful again in her black taffeta dress.

'Go out on the town, sweetie, go by yourself. I just can't do it. I'll stay here and watch television or read a magazine.' There were piles of pre-war magazines in the fake mahogany bookshelves. 'Take some money and go be your age.'

'God, what luck!' said Gueret, literally tearing off his bow tie and shirt stud. 'You've got no idea how awful the thought of going out tonight was?'

'Sure,' said Maria sententiously, in a sarcastic tone, 'going out on the town every Saturday night is like going to the plant every Monday morning. If it's a routine, it's for the birds. Do you realize,' she added indignantly, 'we were going to poison our lives by going to a nightclub simply because we went last week and the week before and were going next week? Why didn't you speak up if you didn't want to go?'

Looking vague and embarrassed, Gueret said, 'I thought you liked it.'

'But why didn't you speak up? I'd have gone by myself. I'm telling you that tonight I couldn't stand it.'

She was growing irritated, close to losing her temper; she felt as though she were bumping into something soft, dangerous, unfamiliar.

'Yes, but you're you,' said Gueret wearily. 'You're smarter than me.'

She accepted the statement with outrageous complacency and said, 'Fortunately,' as she stretched out her legs on a chair, relieved at having evaded the truth, the only sane and plausible explanation: that Gueret would have forced himself to go out with her merely to please her, an effort that, had their roles been reversed, she would have been incapable of making.

A little later, in their neo-Moorish love nest, the two of them, now in their dressing-gowns, pored over their usual papers. Unexpectedly graceful, exotic, poisonous flowers drawn by Maria were scattered over the maroon wall-to-wall carpet; Gueret's papers were covered with his complicated calculations about tropical woods and the cost of their transportation. He made these calculations in three colours, red, yellow, and blue, with a ruler on graph paper. They were figures put together by a careful book-keeper, beautiful to behold but worrisome to evaluate, judging by Maria's frown as she examined them in detail. But at last, for the first time the two of them were one: friends, equals. Maria ended up making him laugh with her drawing of a square girls'-school building with whores at the windows, a river, palm trees. By the light of an outmoded brass and chrome lamp atop a mass-produced end table, these two unlikely, hardworking lovers were absorbed until dawn, planning for their years of triumph and luxury.

It was the first day of summer. It's true – everything always happens at once, Gueret said to himself on his way through the garden, as he saw Maria's flowers, which had bloomed overnight. This thought was reinforced by the sight that greeted him when he went into his room: Maria lying on his bed, the dog next to her.

'He finally got what was coming to him, that stinker,' said Gueret with a laugh as he triumphantly waved at Maria the bottle of champagne he had bought for a fancy price at the Three Ships.

'What's that all about?' she said without moving.

'I've been made head of the book-keeping department,' said Gueret, speaking very slowly, the better to savour the effect. 'You know, Mauchant was supposed to step into Le Hideux's shoes. Well, he put his foot in his mouth and blew it. And so it was me, Gueret, who was promoted head of the entire department! At twenty-seven!'

Maria was in the shadows. He couldn't see her face and he suspected nothing when she said quietly, 'Well, that's something to drink to. Go on downstairs; I'll be along soon.'

The dog jumped down from the bed and followed him at once. Gueret, exultant, waited downstairs for Maria. She seemed to be taking a long time. And indeed, after they had left the room, Maria got up, looked disbelievingly at the posters on the wall – of beaches, coconut palms, tropics – and then, instinctively, at the stove with the stolen jewels. But she looked calm and collected when she went down and sat in front of the glass of champagne Gueret had poured for her.

'Do you realize,' he started at once, 'do you realize I've jumped two steps in one fell swoop? Beginning next month, my salary'll jump from three thousand five hundred to four thousand three hundred francs: I – '

'Correct me if I'm wrong, but you did accept all this?' asked Maria, still speaking in a level voice.

Gueret was stunned. What was she thinking of?

'Of course I accepted! Are you serious? I've been at Samson's for four years, for four years I've been waiting for a promotion. Of course I accepted. You must be joking,' he repeated, deeply shocked.

'And,' Maria went on in her dreamy voice, 'did you tell

them that you'd be head for a few weeks only, that you were going to Senegal to set up a business? You've got to give notice, haven't you?'

Gueret's mouth fell open. He looked at her and uttered, unpardonably, 'Funny, I forgot about that.'

Looking at him, Maria realized that he actually had forgotten about it. The very idea unleashed her fury.

She spat out, 'And it never occurred to you to tell them that their new head book-keeper had killed an old man last month, stabbed him fifteen – no, I beg your pardon, Mr Head Book-keeper – seventeen times. That with the take from the killing you'd planned to buy a lumberyard in the colonies? That Mr Head Book-keeper was a thief and a murderer? What in hell *did* you think about?'

Her look was filled with loathing and scorn, as on the day she had declared war. This was no longer Maria of the Rue des Hongrois. She was no longer his accomplice, she was his enemy and judge. Her scorn was so patent that he got up, as if to parry a blow.

'I don't know what came over me,' he stammered, 'I can't have been thinking. Of course I'll tell them. But, two months as head book-keeper will teach me a lot of things I need to know for the lumber business, things I don't know yet. It could . . .'

He was gibbering, and she watched him deflate with something akin to relief. The shady, dangerous side of Gueret – the murderer and brawler, the one she admired and almost loved – had given way to the solid citizen and careful book-keeper, with his four years' seniority. His pitiful ambitions were proof, had she needed any, of the hopelessness and folly of the love she had caught a glimpse of.

'I'll tell them tomorrow,' said Gueret eagerly. 'I'll tell them I can't, that I'm going away. It's true, I can't. And' – a note of panic crept into his voice – 'besides, tomorrow there's going to be a party to celebrate all that.'

'A celebration!' said Maria, and she began to laugh. 'A celebration, is it? Ha – I'll fix up a celebration for you – in Lille! I'm going to give you champagne, mister – and, for once, we'll go out on the town on a weekday!'

She headed for the telephone, picked up the receiver. 'Monsieur Bonnet? Madame Biron, your neighbour. I need to go to Lille right away. You still have your taxi? Good. I'll wait.' She hung up, turned to Gueret, and said, 'Get the money out of my closet. Take it all; this evening'll cost you a bundle.' She emphasized the 'you'.

When the taxi arrived, the driver didn't dare ask his neighbour, whose needs were usually modest, the reason for her extravagance. All she said to Gueret was, 'Get in front, you're sick.' She shoved him into the front of the car, adding, 'I smoke too much, I'd rather be alone.' She'd settled herself in the back. She was still wearing her gardening clothes, which were even less suitable for an outing than Gueret's everyday shiny suit. With a worried air, he looked into the back from time to time, but all he could see was Maria's granite profile, turned towards the side window. In the rearview mirror he could see the poplars on either side of the road, speeding by and falling back as though frightened that she might have seen them as she passed by.

She had the driver drop them one hundred yards from their apartment, leaving Gueret to mumble some sort of explanation as he paid. Gueret didn't see her until an hour later. She was standing in the living-room, wearing her black dress. In spite of the coldness of the room, he was perspiring in his tuxedo.

'Call a taxi,' she said. 'It's ten o'clock. We're going to the Bataclan.'

The Bataclan was the nightclub to which they had gone for their first night out, the one that had ended so badly. They hadn't gone back since, and Gueret balked.

'Why the Bataclan?' he asked. 'Don't you remember?'

She cut him short. 'That's where I had the best time,' she said savagely. 'They're going to be pleased to hear the good news.'

'Wouldn't you rather go to a new place?' asked Gueret diffidently. She did not even deign to answer, and he went on recklessly, 'And anyway, I don't see what we're doing here. I didn't want to say it in the taxi, but since I'm giving it up, since I promised I wouldn't become head book-keeper, all this is pointless. I'm not going to the Bataclan.'

'I want both of us to celebrate your promotion,' Maria said with a smile. 'Listen to me, Gueret.' He stood motionless, knowing that whenever she used his last name something serious was afoot. 'Listen carefully. If you don't come with me, now, right away, I'll never see you again; I'll never allow you to set foot in this apartment again, or in my house. Never again, do you understand? Never again!'

He nodded speechlessly.

Mercifully, it was too early for the place to be crowded. The orchestra was there, of course. And there were two lovers, an older couple, two hostesses (but not 'his'), and the pal of the bully, the one who had wanted to spare

Gueret in the second round. Also the one who'd prised his fingers off the other man's throat. He was the first to recognize them.

'Well, well, well! So you're back, both of you!' He was surprised, but not hostile, and the hostesses and the three customers turned around and were eyeing them with uneasy respect. Majestically Maria took three steps forward and placed her large black bag on the bar.

'Your rotten little pal isn't here?' she asked. 'Too bad. Al Capone's out of luck. Tonight drinks are free . . . on me.' Opening her bag and putting two five-hundred-franc bills on the bar, she said to the barman, 'Champagne for everybody. My big boy's been made head book-keeper at Samson's!'

There was a moment of indecision while she sat down at a table, followed by the red-faced Gueret. One of the hostesses snickered, the other jabbed her with her elbow to shut her up. Half worried, half smiling – after all, it looked as though the champagne was going to flow freely – the group began to drink, offering little toasts of thanks to Maria. She raised her glass in response, drank, refilled it, drained it, all wordlessly. Gueret, riveted, never took his eyes off her. She drank like this for more than an hour, merely indicating to the barman with her chin their empty cooler or an empty one at another table.

The orchestra had understandably begun to play her favourite tunes, tunes no longer in fashion, that had not been heard since the war. The few customers who arrived later were brought into the picture by the barman and immediately invited by Maria with a look and a nod. They looked curiously at the ill-assorted pair and congratulated themselves on receiving unexpected champagne. They did not talk with one another. Gradually a number of revellers, fascinated by Maria, sat down at her table: first the piano player, then the bully's pal, finally Lola, a sad-faced hostess, one of the whining, down-on-her-luck variety every nightclub seems to possess.

This little world, which seemed bewitched by Maria, gazed at her as she drunk away blindly. She might easily have drunk herself into a stupor, thus ending the evening without disaster, had not the malicious tart – the sorehead, the little drunken one who had unleashed the unpleasantness the first time – arrived around midnight. After a whispered conference with the doorman, she made for their table.

'Well, hello there! You've finally come back,' she simpered at Maria, who neither looked at her nor even saw her, and at Gueret, who was doing his best not to see her. But she headed straight for him and started tugging at his sleeve . . .

'Well, sweetie-pie, don't you wanna dance no more? You look down in the dumps. Come and dance!'

To silence her, Gueret rose to his feet and began to circle clumsily around the dance floor with her as she fired questions at him. He heard nothing: he was completely preoccupied by Maria's aloof, cloudy gaze, which occasionally glided over them without settling anywhere. At the end of a record, as they were about to sit down again, Maria's voice broke out, loud and ferocious.

'Well, the little troublemaker's found her country bumpkin again. Aren't you pleased? If only you knew!' Absolute silence reigned. The hostess and Gueret, who wanted to sit at the table, were stopped by a gesture from Maria.

'Stay where you are, let me look at you! What a couple! What a pity a head book-keeper can't marry a whore! Too bad, my girl.'

The woman started to protest, but something in Maria's tone made her realize that there was nothing personal in the word 'whore', so she said nothing.

'Hasn't anyone told you? Don't you know?' Maria went on, as she noticed the tart's surprised look. 'My big boy there, my Gueret, he's been at Samson's four years now – you know, the Samson plant in Carvin – well, now he's been made head book-keeper! Absolutely! Dazzled, aren't you?' She went on addressing the tart, who, sensing the audience was drunk with champagne and gratitude for Maria, dared not reply. She shifted uneasily from one foot to the other and looked at Gueret, who was ashen-faced and motionless.

'You didn't tell me this lady was your mother,' she said reproachfully. 'You told me she was your aunt!'

She had a penetrating voice, and Gueret found himself the object of attention for ten pairs of indignant eyes, eyes that became increasingly so as Maria went on in a forgiving tone, 'Well, there you are, my boy's ashamed of his mother! He always has been,' she said to the sad-faced hostess, who immediately took her hand compassionately. 'And now that he's had a rise from three thousand five hundred to four thousand three hundred – or is it three thousand three hundred to four thousand five hundred – one or the other,' she added with a sarcastic laugh, 'it'll be even worse. I'll never see him anymore.'

'Come on, of course you will.'

The muscleman, who'd become sentimental with the free champagne, was looking at Gueret with renewed hostility. 'Of course he'll go see his mother, now, won't he? We'll help him remember his mother, won't we,' he said firmly to the tearful revellers. 'And anyway, ha, ha, four thousand five hundred francs is small potatoes!' the woman stated firmly, but her voice was drowned by the murmurs rising from the surrounding tables.

'Children who don't love their mothers should be buried in a common grave,' the bandleader said out loud.

'I may have done a lot of bitchy things in my life, but I'd never have disowned my mother,' the sad hostess swore.

Even the barman shook his head disapprovingly.

When Maria again opened her mouth to speak, everyone was silent. It looked as though no one except Gueret was in any condition to detect the sarcastic overtones of her '*mater dolorosa*' act.

'He'll get married, have children, a TV, retire at sixty; and if he's lucky, he'll be able to save up for a second home,' she said admiringly. 'I'll be a little lonely, but happy for him. I did my best to prepare him for life. I taught him to be honest, to have principles. But you can't teach affection. That's not unusual,' she went on, drowning out the tipsy groans beginning to envelop her, 'it's normal. Boys have to learn to fly with their own wings. And my boy sure has flown high.' She suddenly aimed a sparkling, amused, ferocious look at the downcast Gueret.

Once more Gueret had become the Bataclan's punchbag. Once again he was engulfed in a sea of sarcasm and hostility, only this time his tormentor was no lamp-tanned gangster but Maria, who was having a good time crucifying him in public.

'Stop it!' he said, leaning down over the table. 'Stop all this. Let's go. I've had enough.'

But Maria, continuing her ignoble role, raised her arm to shield her face, as though parrying a blow. A loud murmur rose; the muscleman got up from his chair, stood in front of Maria in a heroic comic-strip pose, and oozed a sentimentality redolent of the provinces.

'He's not a bad boy, but he is violent,' said Maria in a sweet and plaintive voice in which only Gueret could detect the wild amusement.

Suddenly he turned on his heels, cut through the crowd of dazed customers, went up the steps, and exited, slamming the door. He leaned against it for a moment, trying to catch his breath.

He had a headache; he felt as though he could still hear the drumbeat of the orchestra and Maria's pitiless, scornful voice. He talked to himself out loud, swearing at every step. Nonetheless, his footsteps led him to the Rue des Hongrois – stupidly, since Maria had the only key. He took refuge sadly in the corner café, which by some miracle was still open at that hour. He was going to wait for her; there was nothing else he could do, and he prayed that she would forgive him for the ghastly evening she had just inflicted on him.

He waited a long time in the sleazy café, which was kept by a sleepy North African. For no apparent reason, it stayed open till daybreak. Finally Gueret dozed off briefly – just long enough to miss catching up with Maria. A taxi brought her back and she disappeared into the house before he had paid for his drink. She had locked the door and, not wanting to disturb the neighbours, he knocked gently once or twice, but then became irritated and knocked more violently. In vain. Maria sat in the living-room, her shoes next to her on the sofa, a bottle of whisky in her hand, motionless, dead drunk but still lucid. She heard Gueret knock, heard him call 'Maria, Maria' without changing her expression. Nor did she stir when he had climbed over the low wall and trampled the as yet uncultivated garden under the window and crouched by the half-closed blind. From there, unable to see her but guessing she was sitting just a few feet away, he whispered frenziedly, 'Please open the door, Maria, it's me, Maria, I have to talk to you. I won't become head book-keeper. Of course we'll go to the Congo when you want, but speak to me, Maria. Open up.'

She remained motionless in the wan, raw light that filtered through the round glass chandelier. Only her hand moved to fill her glass. She didn't even appear to register, just before daybreak, the words Gueret kept repeating in a voice that had become increasingly youthful, pleading; the voice of a child: 'Maria, let me in. Don't leave me here. I don't know what I'll do if we can't see each other anymore. Who will speak to me? Listen to me? Maria, I beg you. Maria, I don't want to be alone anymore. Open up.'

This went on until morning. When the sun had risen in Lille, the lights were still on in the living-room. The bottle was empty, Maria's eyes were closed, and Gueret, stretched out on the ground in front of the window that was still closed, slept.

The sunlight, a pitiless yellow, slid its rays through the blinds and fell on Maria's ravaged face, her closed eyelids. She opened her eyes, glanced around, stared at the french windows, closed her eyes again for a moment. She then got up heavily on her bare feet and went to the door Gueret was leaning against. She yanked it open and his head hit the casing. He opened his eyes and saw her. They looked at each other: they were both pale, rumpled, alone. Maria leaned down over the man with the glazed eyes fixed on her and said, 'Did I make all this up? Did you or didn't you stab that fellow seventeen times in the stomach?'

He did not reply.

Out of the way, CO.'

For the third time in a row, Gueret got out of the way to let a co-worker by. Going through the door in front of him, shutting it in his face, whistling without answering when he asked a question had become a game at Samson's. 'CO' stood for 'conscientious objector' – no one knew who had first used the term, but it had stuck. After all, Gueret had refused – refused to side with his peers in fighting the management, refused to do battle for his rights, his fellow workers, and his daily bread, refused – for unknown reasons, reasons that were shameful or unacceptable to the others – a promotion.

This game had now been going on for ten days, and in that time Gueret had come to regret Mauchant with his hatred and unfairness. Nothing could have been worse than the sneers of Gueret's co-workers all day long – nothing, that is, except Maria's scorn at night.

She hardly saw him; she did not speak to him. He hadn't dared bring out his plans and maps again. In the evening, his heart thumping, he would remain seated at the table, trying to make up his mind to get up and take them out of the drawer. But every time, just as he was about to do so, Maria would look at him with such indifference that he remained riveted to his chair.

The dog no longer went to meet him at the factory or greeted him joyfully when he returned; it stayed crouched at Maria's feet, also seemingly scornful, apparently preferring an occasional blow from her broom to his petting. Somewhere Gueret had read that fear has an odour. Perhaps it was true and the dog could sniff it on him. At night when Gueret undressed, alone in his dreary room, he would smell his arms and shoulders suspiciously. But it wasn't fear he identified on his skin, it was shame, shame all day for having turned down the job, shame all evening for having wanted to accept it. Although undetectable by a nose, this shame must have been perfectly visible to the naked eye, because even Nicole, when he spoke to her one day, told him to go to hell.

'Well, well! So Monsieur Gueret is willing to speak to us workers,' she sneered with affected surprise. 'Monsieur Gueret must be rich; they say he's expecting a legacy.'

Gueret was stunned by the look of pure hatred

accompanying her words. He looked in vain, through her stupidly ruffled feathers, for the awkward but gentle girl he once thought he knew.

The last straw was that the weather, throughout, was superb, appallingly so. For once Gueret felt relieved when, one week after the 'celebration', Maria, looking mysterious, left him for two days. The very thought of being in Lille during this heat, in the apartment he had begun to hate, filled him with horror. He spent Saturday and Sunday in front of the door at the Wisteria, sunning himself on a cane chair. He was in his undershirt and every now and then, dropping the magazine or one of the books on Senegal he had bought before the catastrophe, he would whistle for the dog, who had also disappeared. It looked as though everyone that weekend had gone to the seashore. He was the only one left in this suburb, seated on his chair like the clod he was, letting the sun burn unattractive patterns on his torso and whistling for a dog who didn't come. Gueret found some relief, even pleasure, in wallowing in his unhappiness. Sunday, however, was harder to bear. Around 8.00 p.m. he began to await Maria's return. He fiddled with the TV, turning it off whenever he thought he heard footsteps. Worried that she would be irritated at finding him there, he went to bed, leaving his blinds open. He lay awake until dawn, when she returned in a car with some character who spoke with a strange accent. Gueret didn't dare go to the window to look out lest she see him and realize he was spying on her. Ashamed of himself, he had to admit he was jealous.

The following morning, as he was riding to work,

zigzagging on his moped he saw the dog on the road
looking frisky and trailing a piece of broken string from
its collar. Gueret wanted to stop and greet it like a
long-lost friend, but he ran into a stone and went flying.
He landed in the dirt with his sleeve caught on the bent
wheel. He swore at the stupid dog prancing around him
and took off on foot, leaving his moped. No one would
lift it in that condition. And to think it was his only toy!

The dog gambolled happily at Maria's feet even before
sniffing around for its plate, but then, finding it empty, it
looked fixedly at her until she caught on. The animal
loved Maria for her serenity and sternness. She said,
'Well now, you good-for-nothing, what are you going to
eat? Where have you been anyway? Did you keep an eye
on the great book-keeper or did you do like me and go off
on your own?'

It wagged its tail as it looked at her. It was attentive:
its dog's memory told it she spoke to it only once a day,
so it knew this would be the last time that day it would
hear her. Actually, four hours later, when Féreol
knocked at the door, she had forgotten all about the dog.

Dominique Féreol was one of the remaining farmers
in the neighbourhood who persisted in actively farming.
His age was anywhere between fifty and seventy –
impossible to tell from a face ravaged by booze, its dry
surface etched with lines of bitterness. Maria looked at
him with loathing and hostility. She had not forgotten
that ten years earlier, when she had just arrived from
Marseilles, she had spent a night with him for a few
francs, which she had then desperately needed. In spite
of her own toughness she had retained a painful

memory of the episode. More than painful, she thought as she saw him smile, leering at her with murky, evil eyes.

'What do you want?' she asked in a level, unruffled voice that for a second deflated Féreol. He had thought to frighten her, but hadn't succeeded. He nearly beat a hasty retreat, but then remembered, hazily, the reason for his visit.

'I want Pacha,' he said, indicating with his chin the dog, who had backed off from the door and was hiding under the stove. The mutt had bared its teeth, but was trembling soundlessly. The intensity of the animal's fear nearly unnerved Maria, and Féreol sensed it.

'That stinking dog's mine, my pretty one . . . That's a hangover from the past, see, that "pretty" business. Let me tell you . . . you're no more than an old bag now, just like me.'

'I'll let you tell me nothing,' Maria said. 'Why doesn't your dog stay at home with you?'

'Because he's vicious and vicious dogs need vicious masters, that's why.'

He went on snickering until he saw, slowly moving towards him, Maria's hand holding a kitchen knife. It appeared to be moving independently, for she was looking him in the eye, motionless. Her hand moved slowly but precisely, straight towards Féreol's neck.

He took a step back. 'What – what are you . . .?' he stammered.

'What were you saying, you bastard. Go on.'

Féreol gradually backed out into the garden. 'I was really talking about your lodger,' he said breathlessly. 'That big shnook, you know Monsieur CO. I wasn't talking about you. You only like smart people, smart ones, not vicious ones, don't you?'

Now that there was a space of three yards between them his courage returned and he swaggered again, as she looked at him with disgust.

'You can tell your pal,' he suddenly started to yell, 'your lousy boarder, that he better bring me my dog by six. If he hasn't arrived by quarter past, I'm going to come and get my dog with a gun, and if the dog doesn't come it can stay here for good; I'll make you a present of the animal – it would make a good rug,' he added, laughing heartily as she slammed the door in his face and, in spite of herself, bolted it.

She looked at the dog, still hiding under the stove, and finally said to it, 'Don't worry, old boy, everything'll be all right.'

In spite of his terror, the dog noticed this was the second time she had spoken to it that day. She even spoke a third time, half an hour later, when she added, 'You're in luck,' as she absentmindedly rubbed it between its ears.

Gueret stood there with his mouth open, not seeming to understand what she was saying to him.

He's stupid! That's what he is, he's stupid! she suddenly thought. He really does look stupid now; he's pitiful and stupid. It made her raise her voice with fury.

'I repeat,' she said coldly, 'that Féreol came to get his pooch, his dog . . . well, your dog. Well, since he asked politely, yelling he was going to come with his gun at a quarter to six, you're going to take this string, put it on the dog, and very nicely return him to his owner. You're to ask him if he doesn't want some money for all the services his dog has performed in this house. You're to say "Thank you very much, Monsieur Féreol," and you're to leave him his dog. Do you understand, Gueret?'

He didn't appear to have understood at all. He looked at the dog, at Maria, again at the dog, with blank eyes, almost sleepily, which surprised her.

'Are you awake?' she began.

But Gueret had already turned around, had reached the door, and was striding rapidly, firmly, at a pace quite unlike his normal one. He was now rushing across the undefined piece of land towards the row of poplars which, five hundred yards away, concealed the small valley where Féreol's farm was located. Maria's eyes followed him for a full minute before she shouted, but too late. 'Gueret! The dog! You forgot the dog!' He was too far away to hear.

It was not decisiveness that marked Gueret's footsteps on the dusty road at this hour; he hadn't the least idea what he was going to say, or to whom, or who this sinister Féreol was. An urge to revolt, to react to injustice, far more violent than any feeling of anger, had been kindled in him. He was Gueret, a decent guy, a good book-keeper, an honourable man – yet within one week he had lost his pals, his woman, his moped; and now they wanted to take away his dog? It was too much!

He didn't know to whom he would say this, but it seemed to him that somewhere there must be justice, an abstract justice waiting for him to lodge his complaint, and that this justice would agree with him, would respond, 'You're right. It really is too much!' There being no judge, he was flying straight to Féreol, not knowing whether he would push his face in or have his own pushed in, of if he actually would do as Maria had said: apologize and offer him money to buy his dog. It wasn't as though Pacha was beautiful or entertaining or even affectionate – it obviously preferred Maria to him, even though Gueret was the one who had brought it to her house. The dog was nothing to look at, knew nothing about hunting, had nothing to offer a man like Gueret. Nonetheless, Gueret thought fuzzily it's my dog. Now they're even trying to take away my dog!

He had reached the end of the path that ran into the road and he stopped for a moment on the sunny slope overlooking the farm. It was an unusual L-shaped set-up, one hundred yards below him. He was the first to see the body on the ground to the left, near the barn – the body of a man writhing 'obscenely', he thought for a moment. Just then a woman's voice on his right began shrieking. The farmer's wife erupted from the kitchen into the courtyard, followed at once by three or four people who had mysteriously and simultaneously realized what had happened. She knelt down next to the strange shape, and it was only then that Gueret saw that the frenzied body was writhing on a pitchfork. The man must have fallen from the loft full of fresh hay, which Gueret could now see. He had been unlucky.

For what seemed an eternity the group remained there, until one of them finally decided to jump on his motorbike and make for the nearest telephone. Gueret was standing motionless when the motorcyclist went by: he was a redhead with bulging eyes, whom Gueret had never seen before.

'Call an ambulance!' he yelled, stupidly, as though he had been on foot and Gueret on the motorbike. 'Féreol stabbed himself with a pitchfork – one prong through his neck and the other through his head! It's bleeding!'

Having fulfilled his function as public herald, he disappeared around the corner, obviously delighted with his mission. Gueret saw him veer towards the centre of town and remembered that the municipal ambulances were not far away. He felt at a loss, undone by the dreadful spectacle. He didn't know what to do with himself now. His feelings of rebellion had vanished. In any event, Féreol, he surmised, would not come to fetch his dog this evening, or any other evening – judging from the ghastly writhings, which were already slowing down, Féreol would be in the hospital for some time. Suddenly revolted at the thought of the feel of the cold metal in his own flesh, Gueret sat on the embankment and lit a cigarette. Ambulances are better than their reputation, he thought, taking his last puff as the ambulance, sirens sounding full blast, went by him. He saw orderlies get out but didn't want to see what they were going to do to the man impaled on his own implement.

He walked back slowly, suddenly in tune with the sweetness of the evening air. He noticed the wheat field undulating in the breeze, the slag heaps sparkling with mica, and for the first time in ten days a feeling of well-being swept over him. He was under the unreasoning but unmistakable impression that his plea had been 'heard' somewhere, that justice had been done – pitilessly, to be sure, but nonetheless done. In fact, now that he stopped to think about it, fate had liberated him from another source of worry. Something inside him made him straighten up and square his shoulders, as though destiny had come out on his side.

From her window, Maria noticed the way he walked. She stood motionless; Gueret saw her but did not stop. He barely slowed down to take a cigarette from his pocket, light up, and then throw the match over his shoulder, like Humphrey Bogart, he remembered. Nor did he slow down when the dog, leaping out the window, ran to meet him, barking and nipping his hands and trouser legs with ecstasy. He gently pushed him away and inhaled deeply a lungful of smoke (which for once he was able to exhale freely through his nose) before coming up to the motionless woman.

'Taking the air?' he said. 'It's nice at this time of the day, isn't it? Cigarette?'

This time he held out the packet instead of taking one out for her as was his wont. She was obliged to get it out herself, and did so with some difficulty, using her fingernails. It took him at least ten seconds to light it, which he did with a weary gesture, saying nothing, just looking admiringly at the landscape. Maria was the first to break the silence.

'The dog – what did Féreol say to you about the dog? You did see Féreol, didn't you?'

'Yes, I saw him,' said Gueret, yawning. 'He didn't say anything . . . and I don't think he'll say much for quite a while,' he added truthfully.

The ambulance was leaving now, the scream of its siren seemed to fly over the wheat field and bounce off Maria's window as though aimed at it. She stiffened even more, turning towards Gueret with a wide look that had become curiously gentle.

'What's that?' she asked. 'Do you hear it?'

She has the voice of a girl, noted Gueret before replying, as he turned away to go up the stairs.

'That's Féreol; he's on his way to the hospital.'

Gueret was lying in the dark, his eyes wide open. The summer breeze drifted through the dark window, drying the beads of sweat on his forehead and neck. Maria was asleep. She had talked with him for a long time that night, and for the first time perhaps as an equal. Gueret, forgetting that this new equality was due to his supposed cruelty, was more revolted than interested by the sardonic account she had given him of her life.

She had loved a man in Marseilles, a tough guy, a man who played hard – a rich pimp she'd lived with for years as though she'd been his wife and who, when a deal had fallen through, had, under police questioning, knuckled under, squealed on his associates, and implicated Maria. That's when she'd been banned from Marseilles. Gilbert, the man who was dealing with the jewels, had been one of René's henchmen.

It was this same René, Gueret remembered now, who had been held up to him as a model. Maria must have been deeply hurt, Gueret thought with compassion, to have lied about him: he must really have deceived her, he said to himself, forgetting that he, too, was here thanks to a deception. But except for this, he had nothing in common with René. Maria was over fifty and he couldn't get along without her. Had he known her at thirty, either she wouldn't have looked at him or she would have made him die a thousand deaths. Contrary to what Maria thought, it was the slightest of Gueret's regrets that he had not known her at that age. At least now she had only him, just as he had only her.

When she'd finished telling the story of her life in a half disgusted, half amused tone, Maria said, 'It's late, we'd better go to sleep. Good night.' And she turned towards the wall.

It was only five minutes later that Gueret, his heart thumping, had dared to move towards the inert body in the bed, a body that he knew would be irritated by his. But he didn't care; that warm body with its face turned away, perhaps in shock, that curt, exasperated voice which so often became peremptory, ordering him to hurry up and have done with it, that voice had effectively put an end for him to years of solitude, unease, mistrust. At this very moment, lying beside the sleeping stranger, Gueret felt liberated from the load of his solitude. His existence was justified. He would be required to do a great number of things to keep this woman, to settle her in Senegal and assure her a happy old age. Now that she had allowed him to return to her bed, he felt totally responsible for her. Even the recollection of her ferociousness during the past two weeks, the memory of her crushing scorn, made him smile in the dark, as though it had been nothing more than the manifestation of childishness on the part of a spoiled young woman.

He slept little and the following morning walked briskly to the Samson factory. His admirer, the young trainee who'd been so disappointed by recent events, saw Gueret approach, walking with renewed assurance. The young man's eyes shone; he went back to his copying and waited for developments. It was at least ten minutes past eight when Gueret entered the book-keeping department and Mayeux, who had taken the job that Gueret had turned down, did not even have time to point out how late he was.

'Get off my back, will you? It's too beautiful a day,' said Gueret in a clear, resonant voice that had not been heard in two weeks.

At noon, Louviers and Faucheux, who had wanted to play their game of precedence at the door of the canteen, were pushed back peremptorily: Gueret passed through first.

The wind had changed and now, instead of attributing his behaviour to lowly mediocrity, his co-workers began to spin wildly imaginative explanations for it. On the way home, Gueret took his moped to be repaired. And so overnight he regained a woman, a dog, friends, co-workers, a means of transportation, and above all his self-respect.

Summer burst out in all its glory and Gueret lived the happiest days of his life. He would go home in the evening his eyes sparkling and say to Maria, 'You were telling me about the day Albert was planning to wipe out the Corsican gang, and you were in Théoule.' Maria would smile, undecided, then reply, 'You're really interested in this stuff? You'd be better off . . .' Then she would stop and no longer insist he go out with women his own age, or go with his pals to a café. She appeared to be resigned to having him at home, dependent upon her, affectionate and obedient, just like the dog. She would go on unwinding the reel of her memory, and without thinking would re-enact certain scenes, laughing as she remembered. She looked twenty, thirty years old, with the port of Marseilles at her feet.

Gueret listened enthralled, looking at her. They would dine very late, after dark, when all around them in the flat countryside the lights had already been put out. Later still, in the room with the rakes, Gueret's naked arm would grope for the light switch.

Maria saw the item in the previous day's paper, which was wrapped around the head of lettuce she had bought. The word 'Carvin' struck her first, then almost immediately afterwards her eye caught the word 'jewels'. She slowly unrumpled the paper and smoothed it out with her hand several times before reading the article. When she had finished, her expression did not change: she showed no surprise, and even the dog, who was always uncannily sensitive to her moods, did not realize it was witnessing the end of their story, the story of these three: Maria, Gueret, and a dog.

'The murderer of the jeweller stabbed in Carvin

continues to deny he stole the jewels. Up to now, no trace of them has been found . . .' The article glossed over the dull story, which now, two months later, was of no interest to anyone. The somewhat confused scenario went like this: a shady character, name Baudoint, who in this case was the buyer, had quarrelled violently in his car with the broker – so violently that the latter had taken fright and fled across the fields towards a canal, the location of which the sinister Baudoint could not even recall; he admitted having caught up with him and having murdered him, but out of anger, not greed. In any event, no trace of the loot could be found. The broker's body had been dragged six miles by the anchor of a barge to the village of Carvin. Even under repeated interrogation, the guilty man persisted in his denials and refused to reveal the cache.

Had it not been for the lettuce, Maria might easily not have read this article, known nothing, and continued her present life. She took note simultaneously both of this possibility and of the anguish the new information was causing her, sat down heavily at the kitchen table, and in quick succession gulped down two glasses of dry vermouth, more for ceremonial reasons than from any real need. She had always known, she said to herself with bitter gaiety, that Gueret had no guts. Reluctantly she went up to his room to make sure those magnificent jewels were still there. They were; but suddenly such splendour seemed out of place in her wretched house. Those lordly gems, robbed of their splash of blood, now struck her as being commonplace, in some way fake, even though they were undeniably genuine. Maria, who until now had handled them with an instinctive respect, was surprised to find herself throwing them up higher and higher, faster and faster, catching them in her hand and smiling at their lightness. Then, laughing, she threw them harder and higher still, until finally, having tossed them up to the ceiling, she turned and went out the door as they cascaded to the floor, appearing quite unconcerned by the sharp little noise they made as they hit.

For a protracted moment she remained at the door to her house, letting her face absorb the last rays of the sun. The dozen or so tired, unhealthy-looking flowers that she and Gueret had managed by their efforts to squeeze out of the unyielding soil appeared to be eagerly stretching their dirty little faces towards the sun's low, inadequate rays.

Gueret turned up at the usual hour, whistling as usual, looking as he usually did. When he came in, Maria's back was turned towards him. She was stirring something in a pot and he exclaimed, 'That smells good,' in his usual cheerful voice before he sat down on his usual chair and stretched out his legs. Maria had not responded to that clarion call; thoughtfully he watched her precise gestures, the nape of her neck, with its lock of hair that was still shiny black. The dog, its eyes half-closed, surveyed them alternately with approval.

'Well?' said Gueret after a few moments of silence. 'What kind of a day did you have? But first, what's for supper?'

'Watercress soup,' said Maria, turning towards him a peaceful, relaxed face, her 'catfish face', as he used to describe it jokingly. The term evoked for him both the blank, mute face of a subaqueous creature, one belonging in another element, and the two-sided, masked face of an alert, mysterious cat. The feline look made Maria's eyes lighter. She looked uncannily like the illustration in an animal book belonging to the young Roger Gueret; he remembered the book from first grade in a school in Arras.

He both loved and feared that look: it usually heralded a surprise. And any event, any new development likely to destroy what now constituted his happiness, terrified him. 'What happened today?' he repeated in a harsher tone.

This apparently aroused Maria from a dream in which he seemed to play no part. She opened her mouth, shook off her air of mystery, seemed to be on the point of crying out, weeping, or biting him. She made an effort to control herself, and her face assumed an expression that managed to be both ferocious and pleading. He pushed back his chair, got up, took a step towards her, and put his hands on her shoulders in a protective gesture quite new to both of them.

'Did someone hurt you?' he asked quietly. 'Did someone insult you?'

She shook her head twice, wordlessly, before breaking away from him and going to the stairs. Disconcerted, he stayed in the kitchen, arms hanging at his sides. When she had reached the top of the stairs she shouted down to him, 'It's all right! I just had a dizzy spell a little while ago – the heat . . .'

Gueret was immediately reassured, as he so much wanted to be, as he so obstinately had been for nine long weeks, the weeks immediately following the discovery of the treasure at the base of the slag heap.

Maria came back five minutes later, completely recovered, her hair neatly combed, her face rosy. For the first time he noticed the light make-up she had on – actually she had worn it for the past ten days. He could have kicked himself for having been afraid of her for even a moment that short while ago. This woman was now his ally, his friend, his 'more than friend', as well as his accomplice. It was no longer by chance or uncertainty or necessity that they lived together, but by choice now, a choice that was slowly becoming what Gueret loved most in the world: a habit. And it was with evident satisfaction that Maria watched him cut up his meat, eat, and drink, as though she had reared him from birth and was pleased with his good table manners.

She looks like a real mother, he thought with some annoyance – it was not easy to forget some of their night-time activities.

When they were having their dessert he spoke to her for the first time, at her request, about his childhood. Until then she had appeared to consider his past existence as nothing but a succession of uninteresting episodes. She had seemed to know everything about Gueret's brief and slow-moving life and to be already bored with it: parents who were irritable or over-burdened with cares, straitened circumstances; mediocre grades at elementary school; unfulfilled ambitions; the death of aforementioned parents; military service, whores, his first love, book-keeping school; his career at Samson's, and so on. Gueret had readily admitted that his own life had been made up of only a colourless and blurred progression, a hodgepodge totally devoid of charm, especially when compared with the amorous, adventurous waltz of her past. He was convinced that, although he conjured up murder, she conjured up adventure.

And yet now it was Maria who was asking him, pensively, 'What were you like as a kid? When you were fifteen, let's say? Were you a good boy or a hooligan? Tell me!' After an initial moment of astonishment, Gueret surprised himself by recounting with delight the dull beginnings of his dull life, and was even more surprised to find her listening with passionate interest.

He was also surprised to find the time slipping by so fast; midnight sounded just as he was finishing the tale of the education of 'Bitsy', the name he had given a tiny orphaned rabbit he had bottle-fed for weeks when he was thirteen, and whom he had succeeded in rearing to adulthood. Bitsy had been Gueret's first triumph over a hostile environment, uncaring parents, and jeering, heartless classmates. Bitsy had the same soft, tan fur as Walt Disney's rabbits. Gueret's eyes sparkled as he spoke about the astonishing, miraculous rescue of Bitsy. In his enthusiastic account he swept the cutlery off the dining table, which Maria, absorbed in his tale, had not yet cleared. As he leaned down to pick it up, a knife blade nicked his forefinger. The fleeting pain it caused woke him up, brought him back to reality, in this case to his lie. His face was a mixture of amusement and surprise as he looked up from under the table.

'Funny, isn't it,' he said, carefully putting the knife and fork back on the table, 'I mean, odd, the mishmash in people. When you think that I didn't even hesitate with the broker: clack-clack-clack,' he said energetically, 'and that at thirteen, I snivelled about a rabbit. Funny, isn't it?'

'Yes,' she replied without even seeming to notice the difference in his voice. It was, after all, a brutal change of topic after the flow of sentiment. 'Yes, it is funny,' she agreed.

Her eyes were lowered when, a little ashamed at having been carried away by his memory of Bitsy, he looked at her, glad to have brought back in the nick of time the subject of the broker. He was unsure where to go from there to keep her interest. He had never before managed to hold her undivided attention for so long. It was now up to her to go on. Maria must have felt this, because she quickly raised her eyes and looked at him with a pleasant smile before glancing down again. She took a cigarette from Gueret's pack and, instead of feeling around impatiently with her hand for a match, for once waited with feminine passivity for him to hold out his lighter.

'What about the position of head book-keeper?' she asked unexpectedly.

Gueret started, then slumped down in his chair. Maria persisted.

'What did you tell them at Samson's? The manager, I mean. You refused . . . what reasons did you give?'

'I said I didn't feel up to it,' Gueret admitted, suddenly blushing at the memory. The biggest humiliation of his life, far greater than that of being pushed around by a motorcycle salesman or beaten up by a small-time gangster, had been saying he wasn't capable of doing his job. But he couldn't tell Maria this because, for her, humiliation meant being capable *of* doing such a job. So he stopped there.

'I see,' she said.

She couldn't possibly see, Gueret thought.

'I see. They must've been miffed. Were you so scared I'd tell all? That I'd spill the beans about your murder? You were afraid of being hanged? Or guillotined?'

Reassuming a dumb, sexless expression – opening his hands and shrugging his shoulders – he replied, 'Well, put yourself in my shoes. I'm not saying you'd have told on me, but you were in such a rage!'

Again she cast him too swift a look, squashed out her barely smoked cigarette, and sighed heavily, as though overcome. The thought that she might feel some remorse at having given him such a fright flitted through Gueret's mind; but at the same time, it was so patently absurd that he began to laugh.

'Why are you laughing?' she asked, without apparently expecting an answer.

She got up, went to the open window, and threw back the shutters. It was dark outside and cool, and even though there wasn't very much smoke in the kitchen, she appeared to be breathing in the night with relief. She must be bored again, he thought. That childish story about a rabbit, when you've had a past like hers, must be like drinking weak tea after a shot of gin.

'If you hadn't found those jewels,' she went on as she looked out on the black night, 'you would have ended up being head book-keeper? You'd have married Nicole, wouldn't you?'

'You're joking,' he started, but she interrupted him without any show of nastiness.

'And you would have lived here in Carvin, with kids and a car and a little cottage. You wouldn't, in the long run, have been unhappy.'

'Why? Why are you saying that?'

She was aloof again, alien, ferocious. How could she suppose even for a minute that he could live happily in Carvin with Nicole! Now that he had all at once discovered adventure and an emotional life! Now that he had started to 'live' with someone – in this case with her! And even if he had never met her, how could she think that such a life – with Nicole, at Samson's, with retirement at the end – could have made a man like him happy? For God's sake, she knew now the sort of man he was! She knew he was choosy about his friends, that he didn't speak to just anyone, that he had to be approached cautiously, to be wooed, to be intrigued – in short, that he needed everything she had given him to make him feel alive and happy.

He was outraged and retorted indignantly, 'No! You know it isn't true. All that's over,' without knowing exactly what he meant by 'all that'. She couldn't have known either – or, rather, they weren't talking about the same thing – when she repeated after him, but in a tone that was far more sad than indignant, 'Oh yes! All that's over.'

She closed the blinds and then the window, thus shutting out the night – and the conversation, thought Gueret dejectedly as he heard the click of the window latch.

'I've bored the hell out of you with all my stories!' he said without turning around. 'My rabbit stories aren't exactly gripping, are they?'

He was already resigned to her not answering him when she came and leaned against the back of his chair. And then, completely astounded, Gueret felt Maria's hand move along his head to his shoulder, slowing down slightly against the nape of his neck in a gesture that was very close to a caress: a gesture unthinkable from Maria, unhoped for by Gueret. His heart stopped, then galloped, while the familiar voice, which was now weary and sad, said, 'No, you haven't bored me. You've even made me laugh at times,' she added gently.

Staggered by the shock of that unwonted gentleness, Gueret took a minute to follow her. In the hall, on the dark little staircase with its lingering odour of mildew, the music of a thousand violins followed him to Maria's room.

Although like a good Marseillais Gilbert Romeut, gangster by profession, read the daily papers, it nonetheless took him forty-eight hours to get to Carvin. He arrived all steamed up, bursting with delight, filled with a secret joy. Without knowing Gueret he hated him and – final episode in his twenty-three-year unrequited love for Maria – he was even jealous of him. Now he was jubilant because his share would be larger, and because Maria had fallen for an insignificant book-keeper. He knew Maria perhaps better than she knew herself. He had guessed that there was more than a common interest between them.

He was somewhat disappointed to hear from Maria that she knew all about it and even more disappointed that she was taking it so calmly, and yet once upon a time she hadn't liked being taken in.

With Maria seated opposite him at the kitchen table, he swallowed the traditional aperitif, and as he began to tell her his plans, he took her hand in his. Uncharacteristically startled, she withdrew it. Gilbert's intentions were pure (oh so pure!) . . . well, he said to himself, even if this Gueret lacked courage, there had to be something seductive about him, to rekindle sensuality and its accompanying choosiness in a woman as weary of love as Maria had become.

'Did you see what I saw?' he asked, in a loud voice.

But Maria cut him short. 'Yes, Gilbert, I saw it. Is that what brings you here?'

Unable to help himself, Gilbert flushed. He felt somehow indiscreet. Putting on a cynical air, he shook his head.

'No, my beauty – it's the money. Surely you don't plan to cut him in now, do you? There were three of us; now there're two; it's neater this way.'

This time he took Maria's hand firmly and kissed it. He had always been the dandy of the gang, the last to regret the passing of two-toned shoes.

'I read the article,' said Maria in the same level voice. 'So what are you proposing? I must have misunderstood.'

'Come on,' said Gilbert in a tone of suddenly outraged virtue. 'You're sure not going to give a hundred thousand francs to a boy who never earned 'em?'

'He was the one who found them,' protested Maria.

'Yeah, but he's not the one who'll get it in the neck.' Gilbert was getting hot under the collar, as though she were raising doubts about an unassailable code of ethics. 'If he'd risked his hide, well, then he'd get the money, a third of it anyway. But seeing how things are – nothing. He lied to impress you. We're sure not going to give him all that money for a walk-on part, are we?'

Maria shrugged her shoulders, but seemed prepared to go along. 'Because "before" when we thought that,' she said scornfully, 'then we would have given him his share? The rules of the game? It had nothing to do with you being scared, no, it was fair dos to give it to him? It wasn't because a man who kills is dangerous? But a man who steals, or who doesn't even steal, but finds something, no reason to be scared of him – is that it?'

'Exactly,' replied Gilbert, who was beginning to think Maria a little odd. 'So, you packing your stuff or not? Are you coming to Paris with me tonight or staying here for a while?'

'What for?' asked Maria in a harsh voice. 'What do you expect me to do here? You've seen the palace, the grounds, the refined atmosphere . . .' She made a sweeping gesture for emphasis. 'Can you picture me choosing to stay here, growing old here, alone except maybe for a grumpy lodger – and that dog!' She pointed to Pacha. 'And the dog would grow old and die before me. You must be joking, Gilbert. I'm getting out, I'm running away.'

'So what is there to run from?' Gilbert asked viciously. 'The books are long since closed on this affair.'

She turned her back on him and went to the little mirror above the mantel. She tidied up her hair, powdered her nose, put on lipstick. This was uncharacter-istic, worrisome.

'We could leave a little pocket money for your pal if you like. I'll even give him one percent, if that's what you want. But as for the rest, little one, we're going to use it to have a ball, I promise. Personally I like the Riviera better than coal mines, how about you?'

She didn't answer, merely shrugged her shoulders and left the room to pack her bag. Gilbert, alone in the kitchen, looked around with curiosity. Same casual old Maria, same carelessness. But, it suddenly struck him, she still had charm. There were cane chairs, a white crocheted lace tablecloth, heavy cast-iron pots and pans: there was no trace of Formica or plastic or modern gadgets. What will she do with her money, he wondered for a moment. She's not interested in clothes, she doesn't like to travel. I can't see her, proud as she is, keeping a man.

By this time Maria had returned, carrying one suitcase. Surprised, Gilbert asked, 'Is that all you're taking with you? We coming back?'

'It's all I have. We'll go by the bank of Lille, where I've got three francs left in my account, waiting for the rest. And as a matter of fact I will leave Gueret a little something. He's been very nice,' she added, looking amused. 'Nice and at times brave.'

'Yeah,' replied Gilbert, 'but only a jerk would make himself out to be a gangster! What a weed!'

'Sit down,' Maria said, motioning him to a chair. 'We've got lots of time. He doesn't leave his book-keeping till six. And I want to say goodbye to him.'

Gilbert's eyes widened. 'Are you crazy? Or just cruel? You want to hug him, then lift his jewels?'

'No, but it would be more polite. You can't know this, but he turned down the job of head book-keeper because of me . . . because of the jewels,' she amended. 'The least I can do is say goodbye.'

Resigned, Gilbert sat back in his chair, lit a cigarette, and asked in an indifferent voice, 'So what's he like? Nervous type? Soft?'

'Why do you ask?' said Maria. 'Are you scared of him? He hasn't killed anyone.'

'Just curiosity,' grumbled Gilbert, furious at being accused of being afraid. 'So what do you think he can do to me? Look!'

He took out of his pocket a stiletto, the only toy he'd kept from his golden years. The dog, either frightened by the knife or because it had heard something, raised its head and looked out the window.

'Why's the dog scared?' asked Gilbert, getting up involuntarily. Maria reassured him and made him sit down again. Poor Gilbert is less frisky than he was at twenty-five, she thought. He doesn't like to brawl anymore. He would never have let himself, deliberately, be beaten up by nightclub bouncers.

She pulled herself up short. Since the evening before, she'd been reviewing all the occasions on which Gueret, in order to impress her, had pretended to be hard-boiled. She could see again, in this new light, the silly little acts he had put on, and even though she tried hard to be angry she only succeeded in being amused and rather touched by his antics. As she remembered the nightclub episode, not once had young Gueret retreated. And she also remembered his triumphant return from the factory and the speed with which he'd given in to her blackmail based on nothing at all. Why had he turned down the promotion? There was nothing to prevent his telling her to get lost and letting her tell her silly story to the police. Why had he watered her flowers when she was out of town? Why had he fallen asleep at her doorstep? And why had he persisted every night in asserting his manhood, insisted that he liked her? What was his game anyway, except that he was not a murderer?

Whatever it was, that game was now over. Whether he had committed a murder, whether he loved her, it led nowhere for Maria. He was not yet thirty; she was considerably older and did her best to look older still. Deep down she had always known she would not go to Senegal. She had known all along she wouldn't be able to stand seeing Gueret, one fine day, walk out on her with some pretty young woman, leaving her alone and plunging her into a loneliness even harder to bear. The few pictures they had conjured up: Maria against a backdrop of banana trees, looking younger, on Gueret's arm; Maria getting into a canoe; the two of them in an air-conditioned bar congratulating each other on their equally profitable business ventures; Maria showing the dazzled Gueret a newly developed orchid – all these pictures would have to go straight into the wastepaper basket along with other pictures of her private life, the colour of which had by now, mercifully, been forgotten.

'You're not bleeding for him, are you?' Gilbert's voice awakened her from her gloomy reverie.

'You think I could have fallen for a young pipsqueak, and a liar to boot? My poor Gilbert! Do you think I'm still at an age to love someone? To lust after anyone?'

'But there's no age . . .' he started, throwing out his chest and feeling for a moustache that because of a dearth of whiskers, was no longer there. Just then the dog started to bark furiously and leaped to the door. At the same time a siren sounded, filling the air around them. Maria said over her shoulder; 'It's only an accident in the mine. Don't worry, we're not being bombed!'

Gilbert was about to be annoyed again that she thought him afraid, but just then the door opened and Gueret came in, his hair tousled and his eyes shining with excitement.

He's not at all bad-looking, Maria thought suddenly, he's no one to be ashamed of. She saw, in Gilbert's eye, the same evaluation – but with an added element of fear. For a fleeting moment, she hoped that for once Gueret would be bold: that he would beat up her former accomplice, take the situation in hand. This wild hope lasted three seconds, exactly the time it took Gueret to hang his coat up carefully on the coat-rack and say, in an unnatural voice, 'Good evening, sir.' Then, turning to Maria: 'I apologize for arriving like this. There's been an accident. We're free until Sunday and I didn't have a chance to let you know,' he went on with unaccustomed formality.

His tone reassured Gilbert and made him laugh noisily. 'Oh you're so very formal here. I'm Gilbert and you're Garot – is that it? Or Guerin? Is that it?'

'Gueret,' Maria's lamentable admirer replied automatically.

This man was supposedly the messenger of fortune, the man bringing the money; but instead of being elated Gueret was filled with panic. He had not pictured

Gilbert as sneering and hostile: he was, after all, being given a third. He ought to have been more pleasant.

'You came by train? A long trip, isn't it?'

'He came by car, don't worry about him,' Maria interrupted in her scornful voice. She had not looked Gueret in the eye since he had come in. Had he not the night before felt her hand on his head and on his shoulder, he would have thought that she hated him, despised him, as she used to. Gilbert darted interested looks around, at Gueret, at Maria. Something wasn't going according to plan. Was it a question of tone? He decided to hurry things along.

'What's it like to stab a dude fifteen times?' he asked.

'Seventeen,' Gueret automatically corrected him.

'Oh, pardon me. Seventeen! Did you like that? Gave you a kick, did it? It wasn't too exhausting killing a big man like that?'

Gueret blushed and lost the last shreds of his assurance.

Maria intervened. 'Stop it, Gilbert. This is pointless. Did you see the paper?' she went on, holding out to Gueret the incriminating page. His eyebrows shot up. He took the paper and sat down at the table facing Gilbert. It was only then that he noticed the suitcase next to the mantelpiece; he looked at Maria, who, with an imperious movement of her chin, ordered him to read.

Gueret read the article, put the paper down on the table, said nothing, didn't look up. He could feel two pairs of eyes boring into him. The silence lasted forty seconds; Gilbert was the first to lose patience.

'Well, Jack the Ripper, what do you think?'

Gueret appeared not to see or hear him. He slowly

raised his eyes to Maria and articulated, painfully, 'I'm sorry, you know, really sorry.'

'What are you sorry about? That you didn't kill the guy?'

'No,' replied Gueret almost inaudibly, 'I'm sorry I told you I had.'

'You didn't tell me anything,' Maria corrected him. 'I was the one who believed it, who wanted to believe it. I ought to have known, just from looking at you, that you weren't the type, that you couldn't have done it. That'll teach me.'

'You're not too mad at me?' Gueret appeared to be coming to life again. 'You don't know how many times I wanted to tell you! What a relief this is. Funny, isn't it?' he added, smiling timidly.

'You sure will be relieved, boy,' Gilbert interjected. 'Listen pal, you were going to get a worker's share in the deal, but now, see, it's out of the question. If Maria wants to leave you something, I told her pocket money's OK, but not much, a couple of thousand or so. You must have a girl somewhere . . . well, a relative, or a pal,' he quickly corrected himself, realizing from the look Gueret gave him that he'd put his foot in it in a quite unexpected way.

'It doesn't matter,' Gueret muttered. 'I don't care. I don't need any pocket money; I don't have a pocket big enough,' he said with a pitiful little laugh.

'Well, OK.' Gilbert kept looking right and left; the situation was dragging on interminably. Action was called for.

'Well, Maria, you ready? Are you coming? The car's a little way down the road. I had to leave it there because it's so slippery. What a place this is when it rains!'

'I left an envelope for you in your room,' Maria said without looking at Gueret. 'You'll be able to buy yourself several motorcycles, big ones.' She went towards the door Gilbert had just opened.

'No!' Suddenly Gueret was on his feet, and his voice made Gilbert stop short. 'No! That's not the way things are going to be. Where are you going?'

'Hey, you fake!' Gilbert had turned around; now that the joker was annoyed, Gilbert was back in his element. 'Listen, you, don't get in our way. She's left you something. Count yourself lucky. But now she's leaving. She's going to live in the sunshine.'

'No!' replied Gueret, shaking his head. 'No! That's not the way it's going to be.'

'You don't really think she's going to stay in this godforsaken hole and keep house for you? Grow up! Maria's going to have herself a ball. And just between you and me, she's fed up with you. She doesn't like wimps. You're not her kind.'

'You don't understand! That's not it at all!'

Gilbert thought he did understand, and his tone became nasty.

'About the money, you can whistle all night for it, Maria and I are going fifty-fifty. Get lost, will you? We're in a hurry. I don't like being in the same room as a jerk. For Christ's sake, get out of the way!' he said, raising his voice.

Gueret was blocking the door. He looked drunk.

'Get out of the way, Gueret.' Maria now spoke up. 'Out of the way. It's all over.'

'He wants his cut,' Gilbert said. 'What do you know? Just look at the dummy! All he wants is money. But he won't get it,' he went on, taking out of his pocket his beloved knife. 'Out,' he said, weaving the blade around Gueret's face. 'Scram!'

'You can leave if you like and take the money with you,' Gueret said in a toneless voice, 'but not Maria. Maria's staying with me. She told me she would. We're going to Senegal. I know all the shipping tables by heart. We've been planning it for months, haven't we, Maria? Now get out!'

'You want me to take the money and leave you Maria?' Gilbert sounded shocked, though he rather liked the idea. If Maria agreed . . . it would be quite a deal for him. But she was frowning and breathing fast, a sign she was getting annoyed, that things had to be hurried up a bit.

'For the last time, will you get out the way? I'm leaving. So's Maria. Can't you understand, you little bastard?'

Maria took a step towards the door. Gueret, upset as he was, might have let her go, had not Gilbert made an ill-advised gesture of courtesy in opening the door for her – in doing so he pushed Gueret against the wall. With a convulsive movement, Gueret grabbed him by the neck and, beside himself with fury, began to shake him.

'You're not going to take Maria!' he said as Gilbert dangled from his hands. 'Maria's going to stay with me, with or without the money. We don't give a damn about the money. She's staying with us, with the dog and me. We both love her. D'you understand? I love Maria,' he said furiously, 'and I don't give a damn if we're in Senegal or the coal pits. It's Maria I want, Maria and the dog. That's all.'

'Let go of me!' Gilbert was suffocating. He was turning white, he was starting to resemble the guy at the nightclub. And as in the nightclub, Gueret did not even notice.

'Let go of him, Gueret,' Maria said, curtly. 'Let him go!'

'And Maria loves us, too,' he went on, banging Gilbert's head against the wall. 'She can't live without us either. Do you understand?'

But Gilbert had not understood at all. The only thing he understood was that he was going to die if this big idiot didn't loosen his grip. He felt around until he was able to get his fingers back on his knife and, slowly but skilfully, stuck it in Gueret's stomach. For a moment Gueret appeared not to notice.

'For God's sake, let him go!' said Maria, who had seen nothing. She simply thought she had been obeyed when she saw Gilbert, released, retreating three steps towards her. Then she caught sight of the stain on Gueret's trousers, his look of surprise. She saw him fall across the door. The dog went up to him, sniffing, looking bewildered.

'Shit!' Gilbert said in a low voice. 'Shit! Did he ever scare me!'

'Call the ambulance,' Maria merely replied.

She had seen where the blood was coming from and already knew what the outcome would be.

The ambulance came quickly, almost too quickly for Gueret, who was not yet in pain and who was more surprised than frightened at the sight of the blood spurting out. Maria had put her coat under his head, a sure sign that she was not leaving; that was all that mattered. He felt relieved. He'd been worried sick, certainly, but now she knew everything; she would stay with him and whether or not they had the money, they would have a marvellously happy life together. So he was most co-operative with the young intern and the ambulance drivers and he had no difficulty pretending it was an accident.

'It's the spleen,' said the young doctor, growing pale and moving faster.

Gueret lay half-reclined in the ambulance. He could still see the sky, the fields, the top of the slag heap, and especially, in the foreground, Maria's face looking at him with a strange but tender expression.

'You'll be here when I come back, won't you?' He was short of breath. He felt pale and cold. What a stupid fight; he had always known it was stupid to get into a fight.

'Yes, I'll be here.'

He was now settled in the ambulance. The intern was close to him, taking his pulse, looking at Maria, whose eyebrows were raised questioningly. Gueret, uncomprehending, saw the intern shake his head from left to right, his eyes lowered. Gilbert appeared to have lost his nerve and was running away towards his car. An orderly started to close one of the ambulance doors and the sky shrank away as Gueret looked between the two slabs of white-painted metal. He raised his hand to stop him, and the orderly obeyed out of sheer kindness, though they were in such a hurry.

'You'll wait for me, you promise?' he asked in a strangely hoarse voice. 'You will wait, Maria? You swear?'

Maria leaned down a little farther in the semi-darkness of the ambulance. He could see her face looking large, unreal. A face so quick to show scorn and yet so tender when she's not paying attention, he said to himself. His side was starting to hurt.

'I'll wait for you for the rest of my life, you poor little bastard,' she said tonelessly.

The orderly closed the door and all Gueret could see was the white wall that separated him from her.

Though it was useless, the ambulance took off like an arrow, sirens screaming. The dog ran after it for a while, then stopped two hundred yards down the road when it realized it couldn't keep up. It stayed in the middle of the road looking first in the direction of the town, then towards Maria. She stood motionless in the very place where Gueret once had seen her, in her black dress, waiting for him. She didn't stir.

The dog hesitated, looked again down the road, then at her, and suddenly took off at a trot, in another direction.

STAR BOOKS BESTSELLERS

FICTION

EMBRACE THE WIND	Ashley Carter	£2.25*
AGAINST ALL GODS	Ashley Carter	£1.95*
THE OFFICERS WIVES	Thomas Fleming	£3.25*
DREAMS OF GLORY	Thomas Fleming	£2.50*
THE CARDINAL SINS	Andrew M.Greeley	£1.95*
THY BROTHERS WIFE	Andrew M.Greeley	£1.95*
LORD OF THE DANCE	Andrew M.Greeley	£2.50*
DEAR STRANGER	Catherine Kidwell	£1.95*
DAYS OF ETERNITY	Gordon Glasco	£2.50*
THE GARMENT	Catherine Cookson	£1.60
HANNAH MASSEY	Catherine Cookson	£1.95
SLINKY JANE	Catherine Cookson	£1.60
LETS KEEP IN TOUCH	Elaine Bissell	£2.50
FALCON CREST	Patrick Mann	£2.25

STAR Books are obtainable from many booksellers and newsagents. If you have any difficulty tick the titles you want and fill in the form below.

Name _____

Address _____

_____

STAR BOOKS BESTSELLERS

FICTION

THE PAINTED LADY	Francoise Sagan	£2.25*
THE STILL STORM	Francoise Sagan	£1.95*
THE UNMADE BED	Francoise Sagan	£1.95*
INCIDENTAL MUSIC	Francoise Sagan	£2.00*
TRADE OFFS	Jane Adams	£2.50*
GARLAND OF WAR	Tessa Barclay	£1.95
A SOWER WENT FORTH	Tessa Barclay	£2.25
THE STONY PLACES	Tessa Barclay	£2.25
HARVEST OF THORNS	Tessa Barclay	£2.25
THE GOOD GROUND	Tessa Barclay	£1.95
THE BREADWINNER	Tessa Barclay	£1.95
SOUTHERN WOMEN	Lois Battle	£2.95
WAR BRIDES	Lois Battle	£2.75
A DARKLING MOON	Ashley Carter	£2.50*
THE OUTLANDERS	Ashley Carter	£2.50*

STAR Books are obtainable from many booksellers and newsagents. If you have any difficulty tick the titles you want and fill in the form below.

Name _____

Address _____

_____

Send to: Star Books Cash Sales, P.O. Box 11, Falmouth, Cornwall, TR10 9EN.

Please send a cheque or postal order to the value of the cover price plus:
UK: 55p for the first book, 22p for the second book and 14p for each additional book ordered to the maximum charge of £1.75.

BFPO and EIRE: 55p for the first book, 22p for the second book, 14p per copy for the next 7 books, thereafter 8p per book.

OVERSEAS: £1.00 for the first book and 25p per copy for each additional book.

While every effort is made to keep prices low, it is sometimes necessary to increase prices at short notice. Star Books reserve the right to show new retail prices on covers which may differ from those advertised in the text or elsewhere.

*NOT FOR SALE IN CANADA

STAR BOOKS BESTSELLERS

FICTION

VOICE OF THE NIGHT	D.R.Koontz	£2.25*
DARKNESS COMES	D.R.Koontz	£2.50*
WHISPERS	D.R.Koontz	£2.25*
NIGHT CHILLS	D.R.Koontz	£2.60*
SHATTERED	D.R.Koontz	£1.80*
PHANTOMS	D.R.Koontz	£1.95*
CHASE	D.R.Koontz	£1.95*
POST OFFICE	Charles Bukowski	£1.80*
DANCEHALL	Bernard F.Conners	£2.25*
GOLD COAST	Elmore Leonard	£1.95*
SPLIT IMAGES	Elmore Leonard	£1.95*
ALL OR NOTHING	Stephen Longstreet	£2.50*
THE BODY	Richard Ben Sapir	£2.50*
HEADHUNTER	Michael Slade	£2.75*
THE LONG AFTERNOON	Ursula Zilinsky	£2.75*
BIRTHRIGHT	Colin Sharp	£1.95*